POKÉMON™ X•Y

STORY
Hidenori Xsaka

ART
Satoshi Yamamoto

5

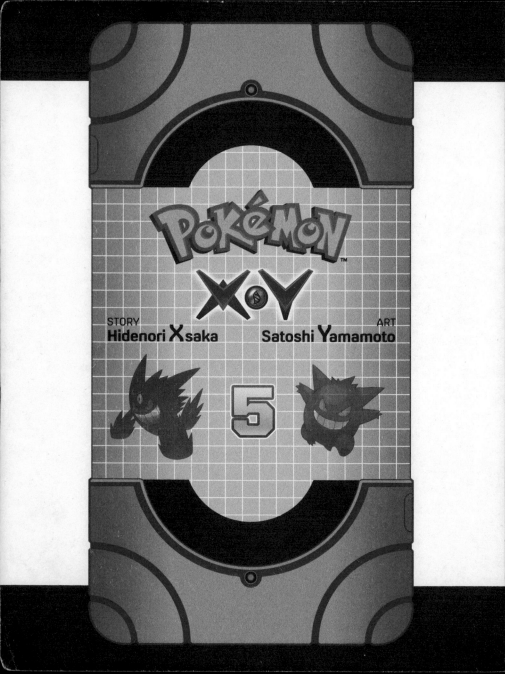

CHARACTERS

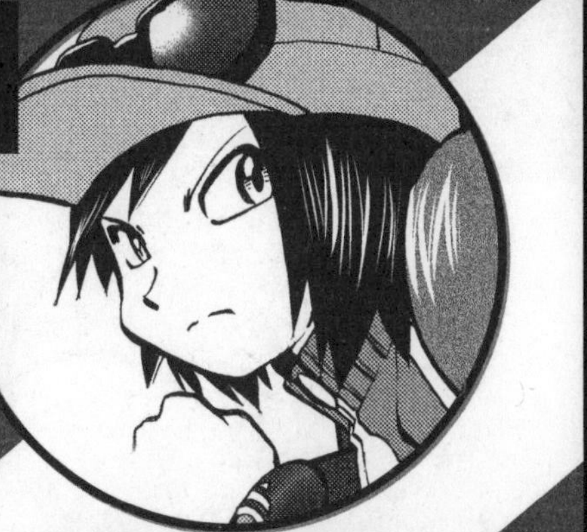

X

The main character of this chapter, and one of five close childhood friends. He was once a highly skilled Trainer who even won the Junior Pokémon Battle Tournament, but now...

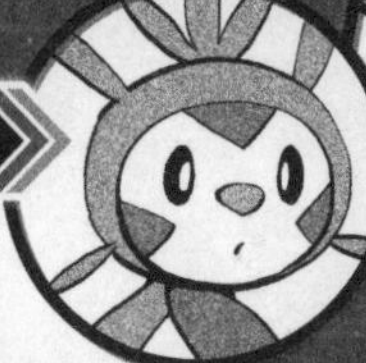

MARISSO

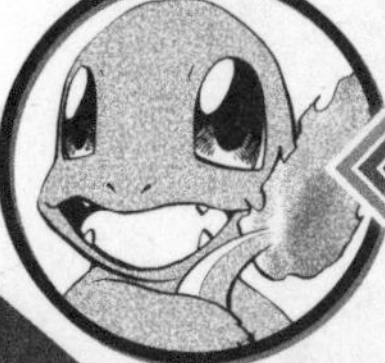

SALAMÈ

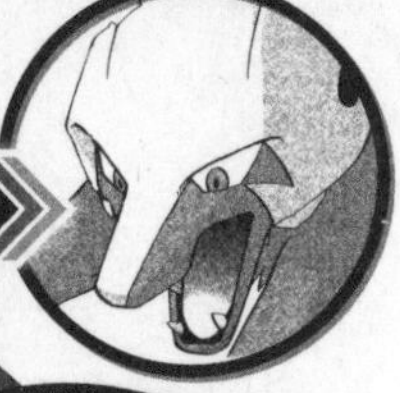

ÉLEC

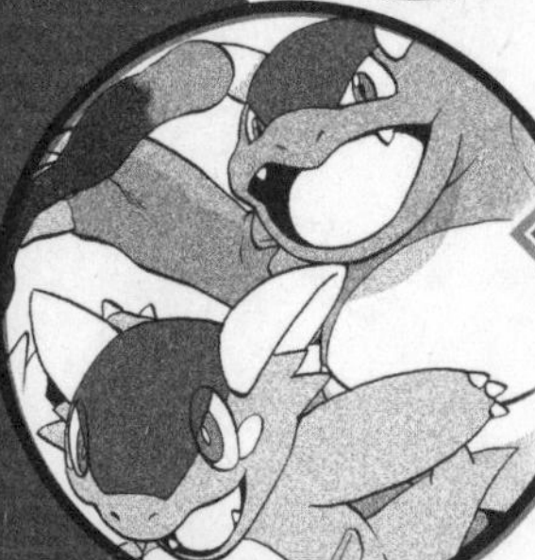

KANGA & LI'L KANGA

X's longtime Pokémon partners with whom he won the Junior Tournament.

OUR STORY THUS FAR...

In Vaniville Town in the Kalos Region, X is a Pokémon Trainer child prodigy. But then he falls into a depression and hides in his room avoiding everyone. A sudden attack by Legendary Pokémon Xerneas and Yveltal, controlled by Team Flare, forces X outside. Now he and his closest childhood friends—Y, Trevor, Tierno and Shauna—are on the run. X has a ring that Mega Evolves Pokémon and Team Flare wants to steal it! On their journey through Lumiose City, Route 5, and Camphrier Town, X adds a Chespin (Marisso) to his official team, as well as a Charmander (Salamè) and a Manectric (Élec) who Mega Evolves. With the help of a computer technician named Cassius, our friends continue on their way...!

MEET THE

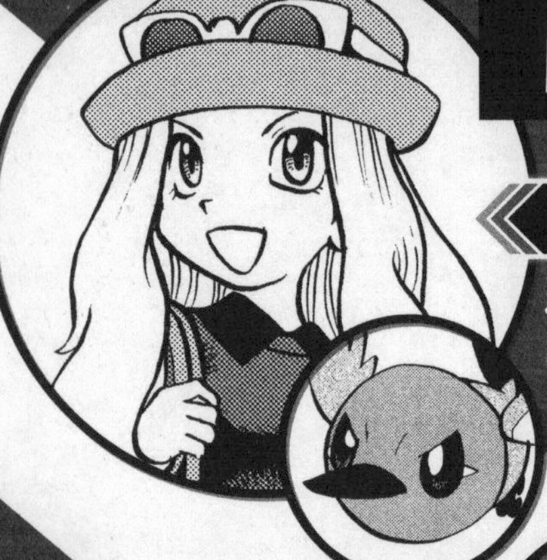

Y

X's best friend, a Sky Trainer trainee. Her full name is Yvonne Gabena.

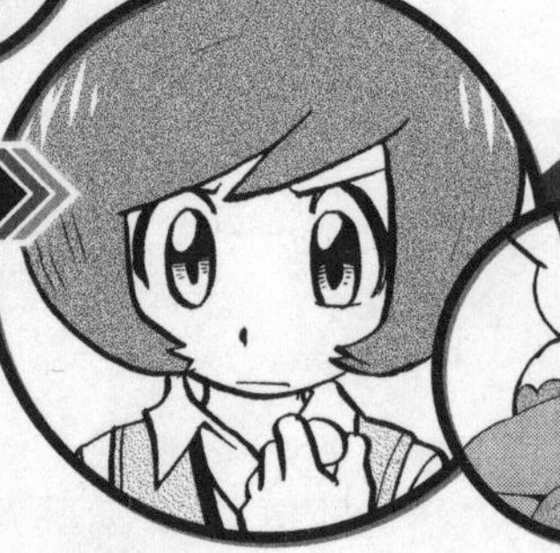

TREVOR

One of the five friends. A quiet boy who hopes to become a fine Pokémon Researcher one day.

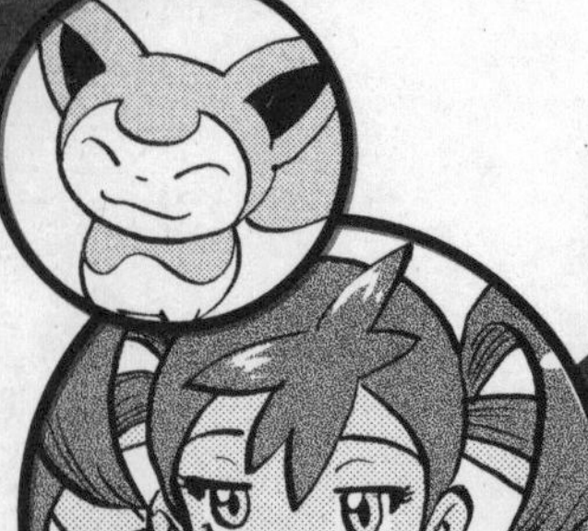

SHAUNA

One of the five friends. Her dream is to become a Furfrou Groomer. She is quick to speak her mind.

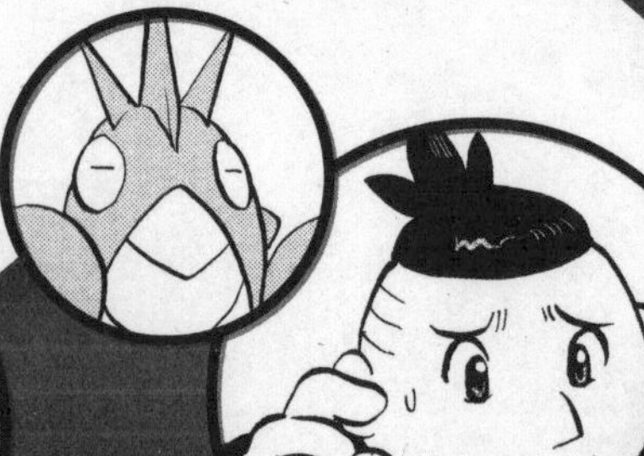

TIERNO

One of the five friends. A big boy with an even bigger heart. He is currently training to become a dancer.

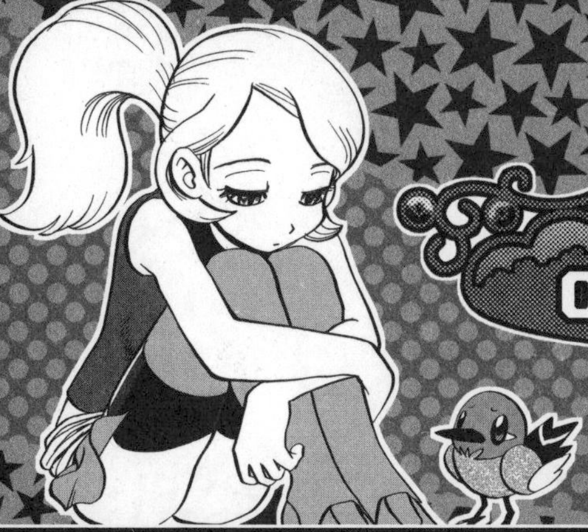

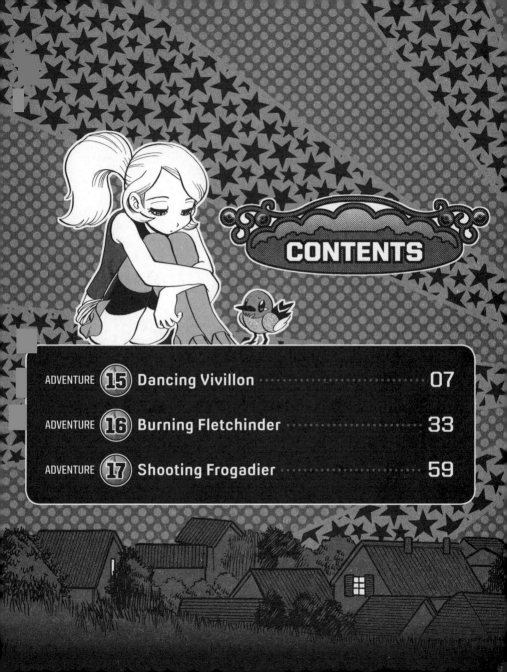

CONTENTS

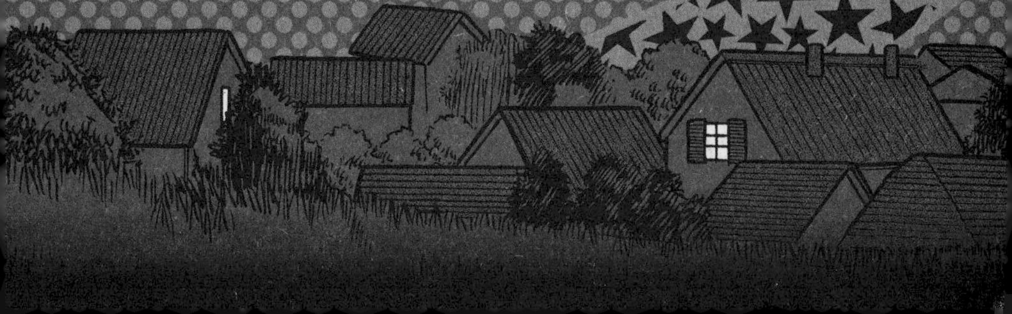

Adventure 15 Dancing Vivillon

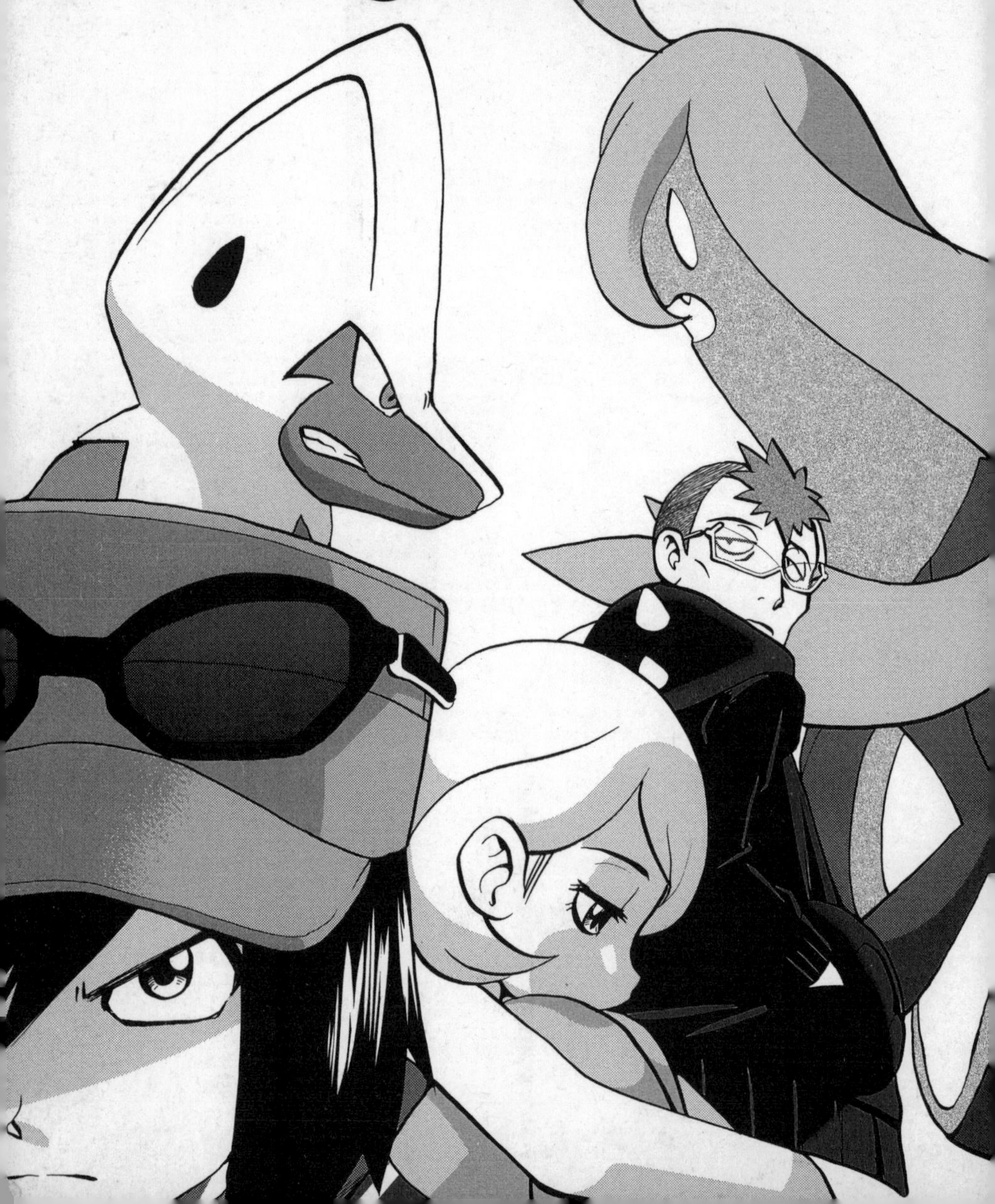

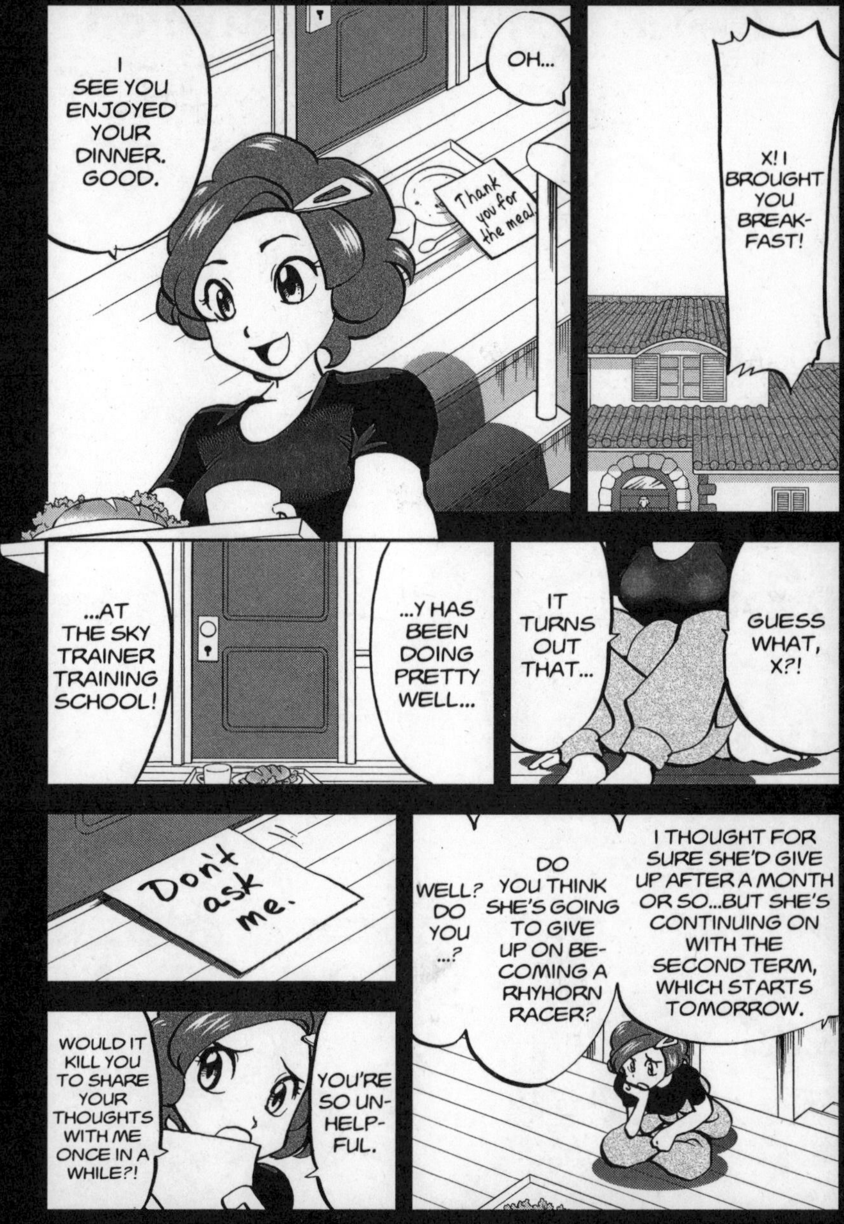
X! I BROUGHT YOU BREAKFAST!
OH...
I SEE YOU ENJOYED YOUR DINNER. GOOD.
Thank you for the meal.
GUESS WHAT, X?!
IT TURNS OUT THAT...
...Y HAS BEEN DOING PRETTY WELL...
...AT THE SKY TRAINER TRAINING SCHOOL!
I THOUGHT FOR SURE SHE'D GIVE UP AFTER A MONTH OR SO...BUT SHE'S CONTINUING ON WITH THE SECOND TERM, WHICH STARTS TOMORROW.
DO YOU THINK SHE'S GOING TO GIVE UP ON BE-COMING A RHYHORN RACER?
WELL? DO YOU ...?
Don't ask me.
YOU'RE SO UN-HELP-FUL.
WOULD IT KILL YOU TO SHARE YOUR THOUGHTS WITH ME ONCE IN A WHILE?!

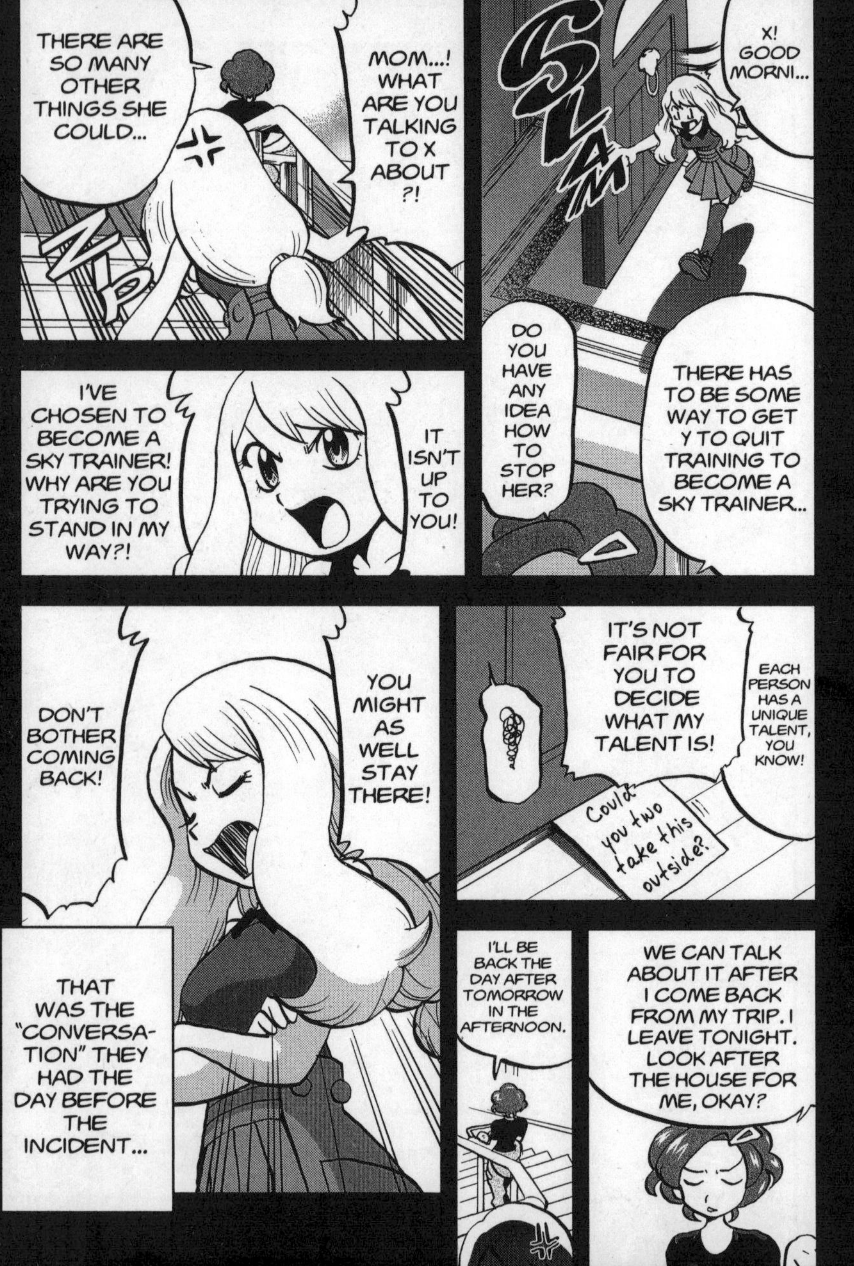
X! GOOD MORNI...
SLAM
MOM...! WHAT ARE YOU TALKING TO X ABOUT?!
THERE ARE SO MANY OTHER THINGS SHE COULD...
NIP
THERE HAS TO BE SOME WAY TO GET Y TO QUIT TRAINING TO BECOME A SKY TRAINER...
DO YOU HAVE ANY IDEA HOW TO STOP HER?
IT ISN'T UP TO YOU!
I'VE CHOSEN TO BECOME A SKY TRAINER! WHY ARE YOU TRYING TO STAND IN MY WAY?!
EACH PERSON HAS A UNIQUE TALENT, YOU KNOW!
IT'S NOT FAIR FOR YOU TO DECIDE WHAT MY TALENT IS!
Could you two take this outside?
WE CAN TALK ABOUT IT AFTER I COME BACK FROM MY TRIP. I LEAVE TONIGHT. LOOK AFTER THE HOUSE FOR ME, OKAY?
I'LL BE BACK THE DAY AFTER TOMORROW IN THE AFTERNOON.
YOU MIGHT AS WELL STAY THERE!
DON'T BOTHER COMING BACK!
THAT WAS THE "CONVERSATION" THEY HAD THE DAY BEFORE THE INCIDENT...

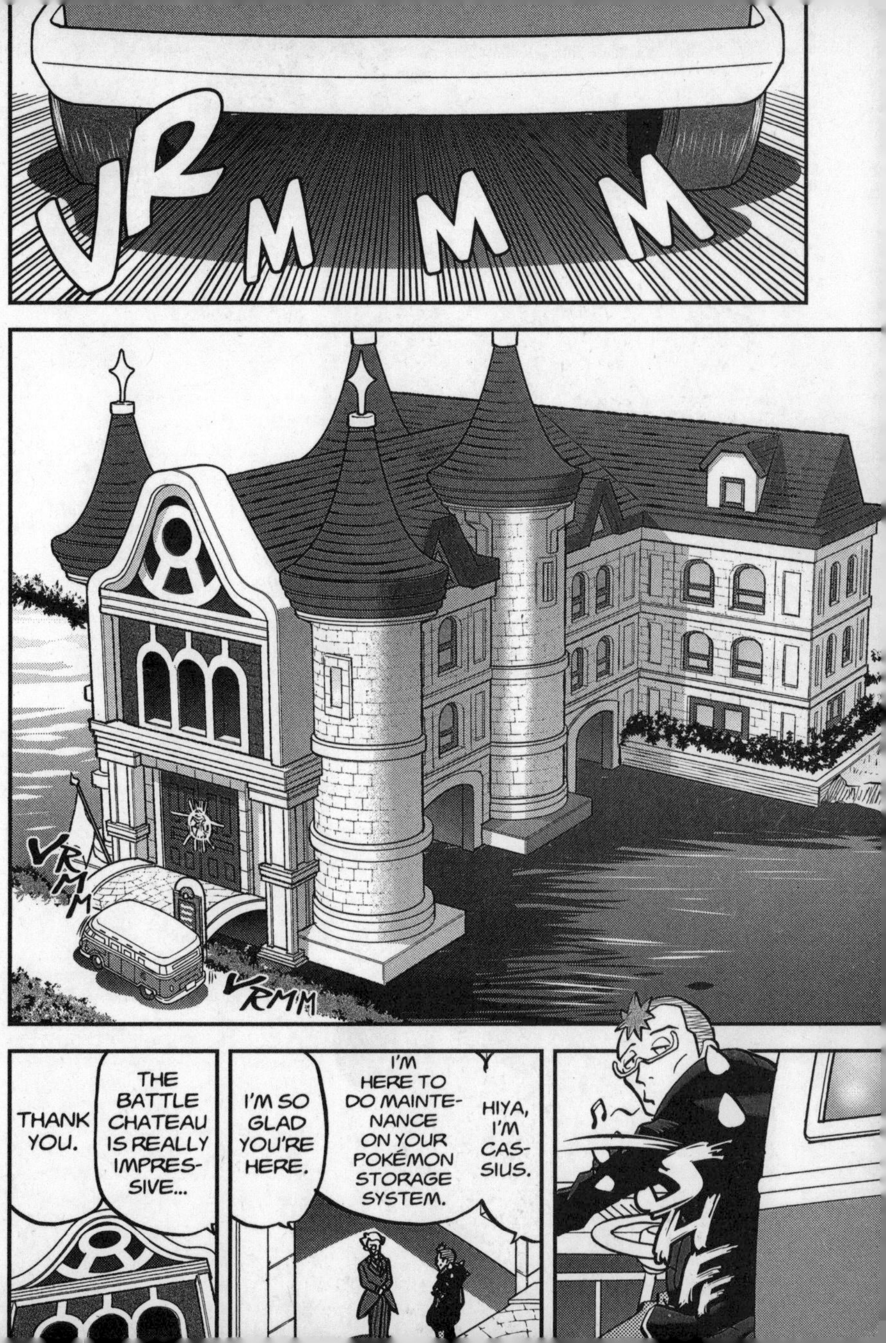
VRMMM
VRMMM
VRMMM
SHFF
HIYA, I'M CASSIUS.
I'M HERE TO DO MAINTENANCE ON YOUR POKÉMON STORAGE SYSTEM.
I'M SO GLAD YOU'RE HERE.
THE BATTLE CHATEAU IS REALLY IMPRESSIVE...
THANK YOU.

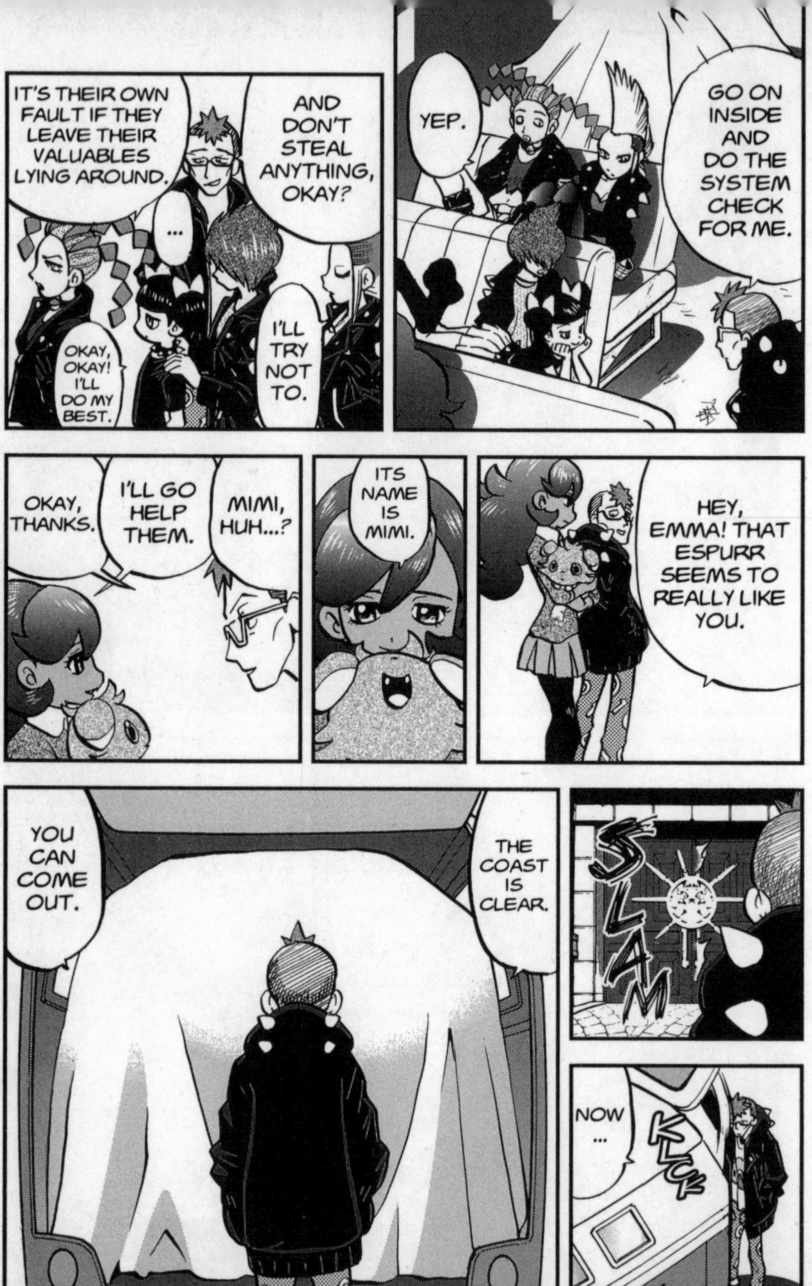
GO ON INSIDE AND DO THE SYSTEM CHECK FOR ME.
YEP.
AND DON'T STEAL ANYTHING, OKAY?
IT'S THEIR OWN FAULT IF THEY LEAVE THEIR VALUABLES LYING AROUND.
...
I'LL TRY NOT TO.
OKAY, OKAY! I'LL DO MY BEST.
HEY, EMMA! THAT ESPURR SEEMS TO REALLY LIKE YOU.
ITS NAME IS MIMI.
MIMI, HUH...?
I'LL GO HELP THEM.
OKAY, THANKS.
SLAM
KLICK
NOW ...
THE COAST IS CLEAR.
YOU CAN COME OUT.

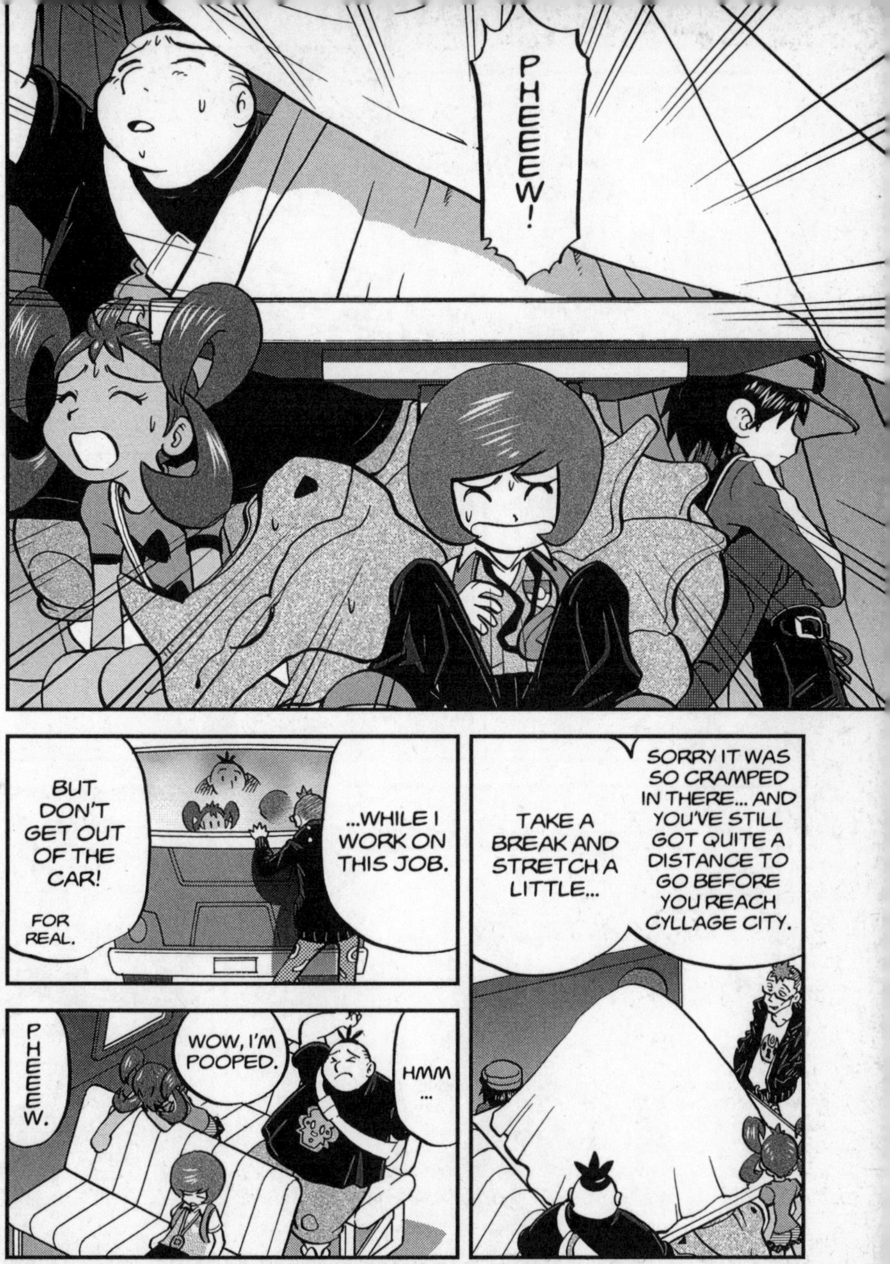
PHEEEW!
SORRY IT WAS SO CRAMPED IN THERE... AND YOU'VE STILL GOT QUITE A DISTANCE TO GO BEFORE YOU REACH CYLLAGE CITY.
TAKE A BREAK AND STRETCH A LITTLE...
...WHILE I WORK ON THIS JOB.
BUT DON'T GET OUT OF THE CAR!
FOR REAL.
HMM ...
WOW, I'M POOPED.
PHEEEEW.

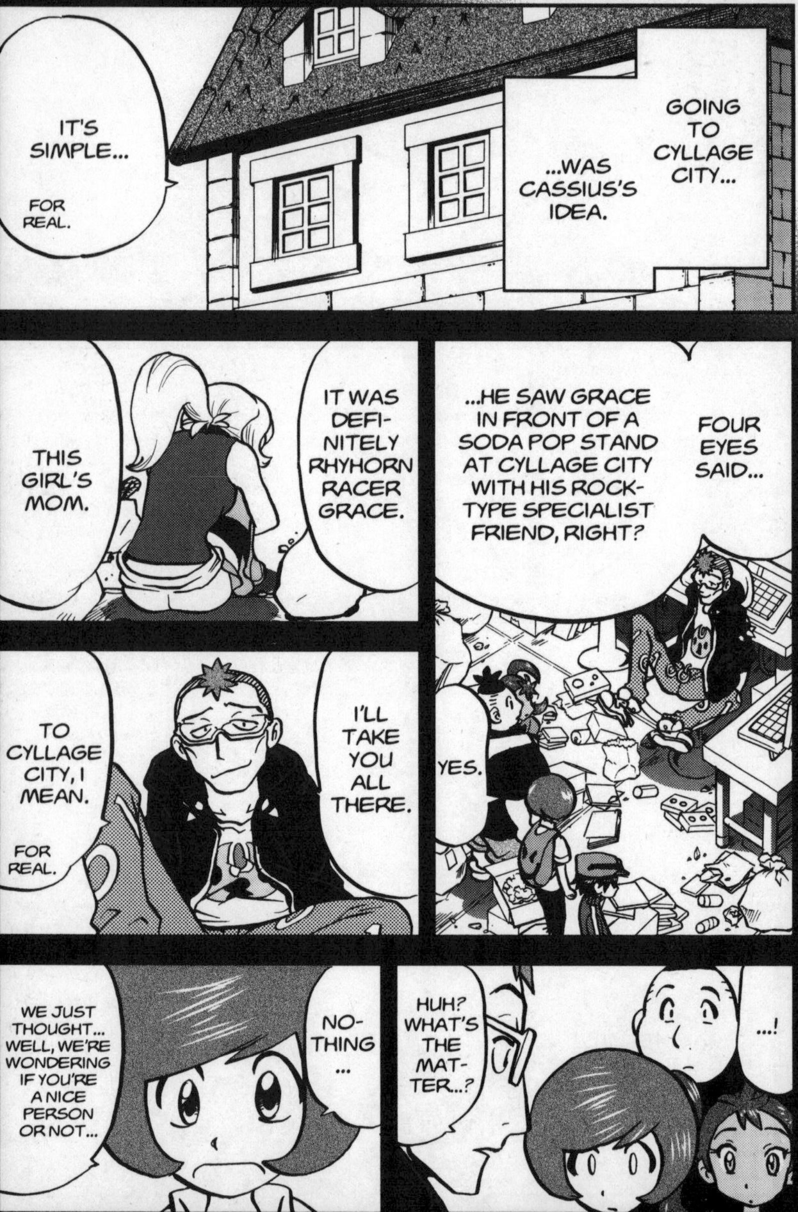
GOING TO CYLLAGE CITY...
...WAS CASSIUS'S IDEA.
IT'S SIMPLE...
FOR REAL.
FOUR EYES SAID...
...HE SAW GRACE IN FRONT OF A SODA POP STAND AT CYLLAGE CITY WITH HIS ROCK-TYPE SPECIALIST FRIEND, RIGHT?
YES.
IT WAS DEFI-NITELY RHYHORN RACER GRACE.
THIS GIRL'S MOM.
I'LL TAKE YOU ALL THERE.
TO CYLLAGE CITY, I MEAN.
FOR REAL.
...!
HUH? WHAT'S THE MAT-TER...?
NO-THING...
WE JUST THOUGHT... WELL, WE'RE WONDERING IF YOU'RE A NICE PERSON OR NOT...

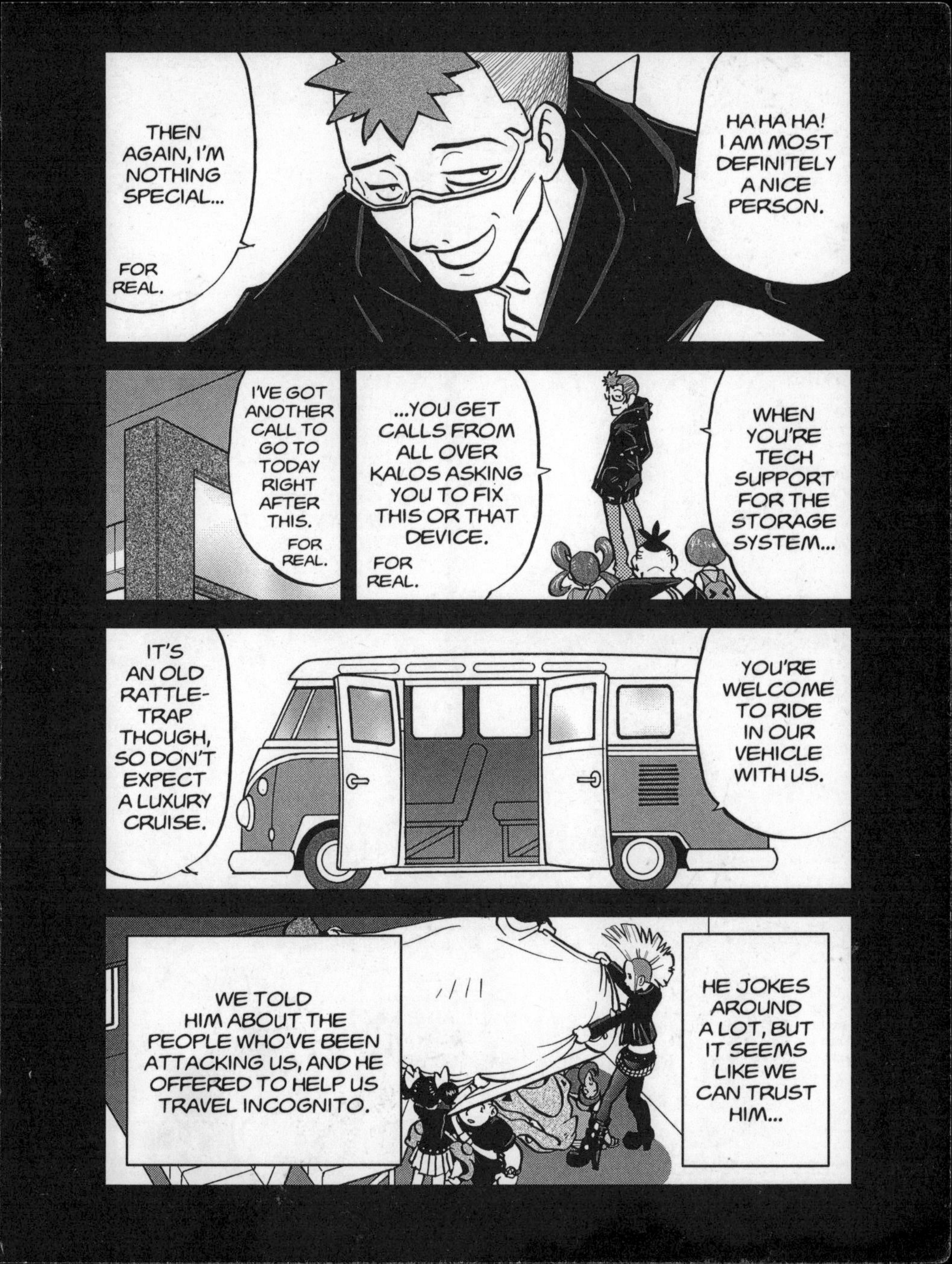
HA HA HA! I AM MOST DEFINITELY A NICE PERSON.
THEN AGAIN, I'M NOTHING SPECIAL...
FOR REAL.
WHEN YOU'RE TECH SUPPORT FOR THE STORAGE SYSTEM...
...YOU GET CALLS FROM ALL OVER KALOS ASKING YOU TO FIX THIS OR THAT DEVICE.
FOR REAL.
I'VE GOT ANOTHER CALL TO GO TO TODAY RIGHT AFTER THIS.
FOR REAL.
YOU'RE WELCOME TO RIDE IN OUR VEHICLE WITH US.
IT'S AN OLD RATTLE-TRAP THOUGH, SO DON'T EXPECT A LUXURY CRUISE.
HE JOKES AROUND A LOT, BUT IT SEEMS LIKE WE CAN TRUST HIM...
WE TOLD HIM ABOUT THE PEOPLE WHO'VE BEEN ATTACKING US, AND HE OFFERED TO HELP US TRAVEL INCOGNITO.

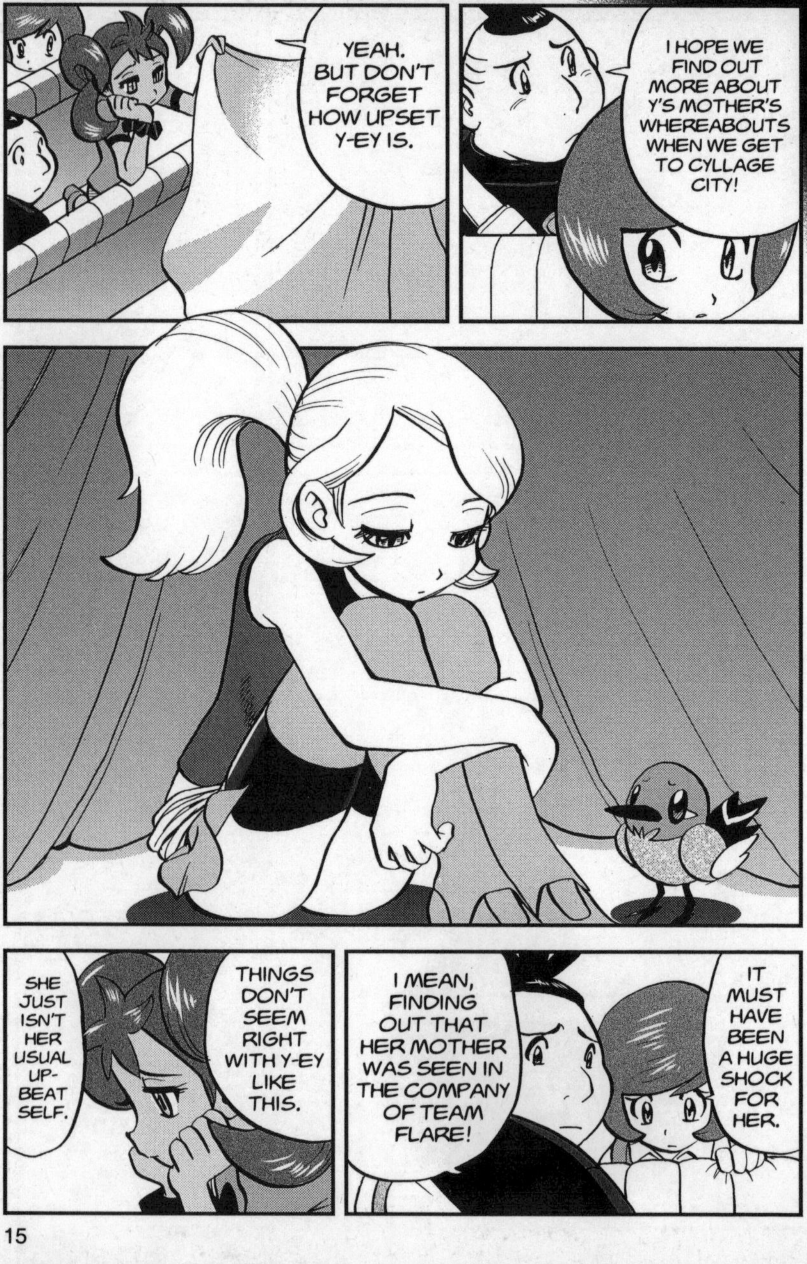
I HOPE WE FIND OUT MORE ABOUT Y'S MOTHER'S WHEREABOUTS WHEN WE GET TO CYLLAGE CITY!
YEAH. BUT DON'T FORGET HOW UPSET Y-EY IS.
IT MUST HAVE BEEN A HUGE SHOCK FOR HER.
I MEAN, FINDING OUT THAT HER MOTHER WAS SEEN IN THE COMPANY OF TEAM FLARE!
THINGS DON'T SEEM RIGHT WITH Y-EY LIKE THIS.
SHE JUST ISN'T HER USUAL UP-BEAT SELF.

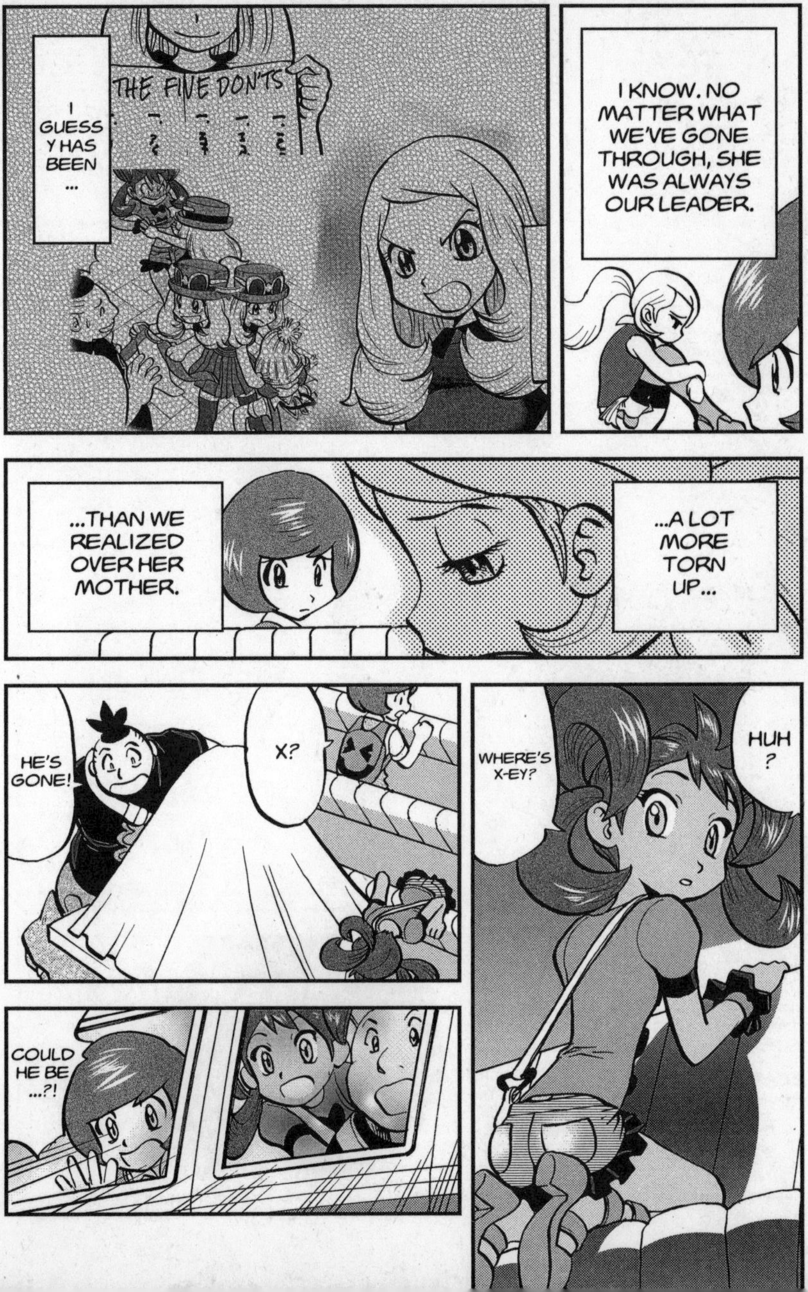
I KNOW. NO MATTER WHAT WE'VE GONE THROUGH, SHE WAS ALWAYS OUR LEADER.
THE FIVE DON'TS
I GUESS Y HAS BEEN ...
...A LOT MORE TORN UP...
...THAN WE REALIZED OVER HER MOTHER.
HUH ?
WHERE'S X-EY?
X?
HE'S GONE!
COULD HE BE ...?!

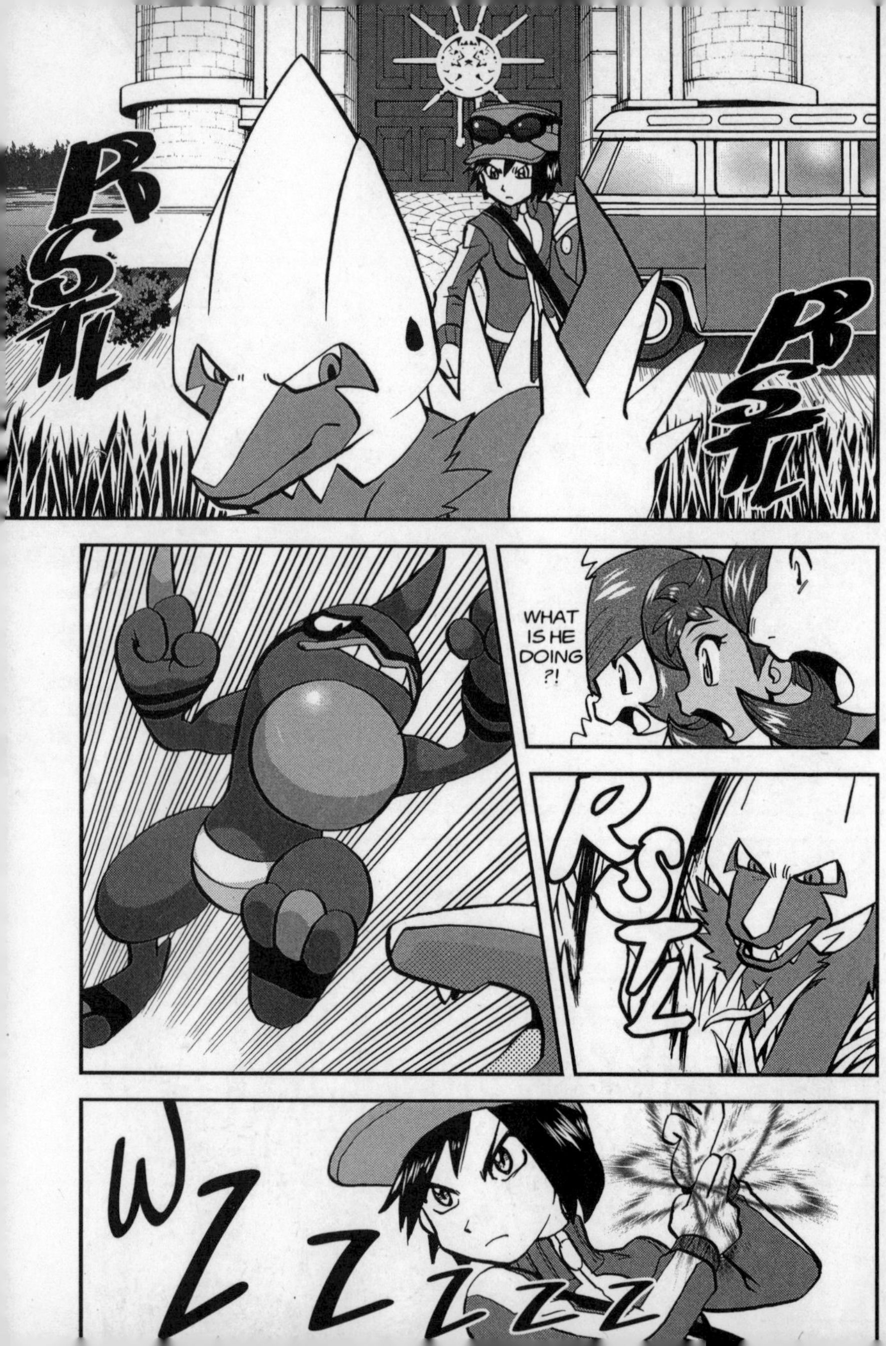
RSTL
RSTL
WHAT IS HE DOING?!
RSTL
WZZZZZZZ

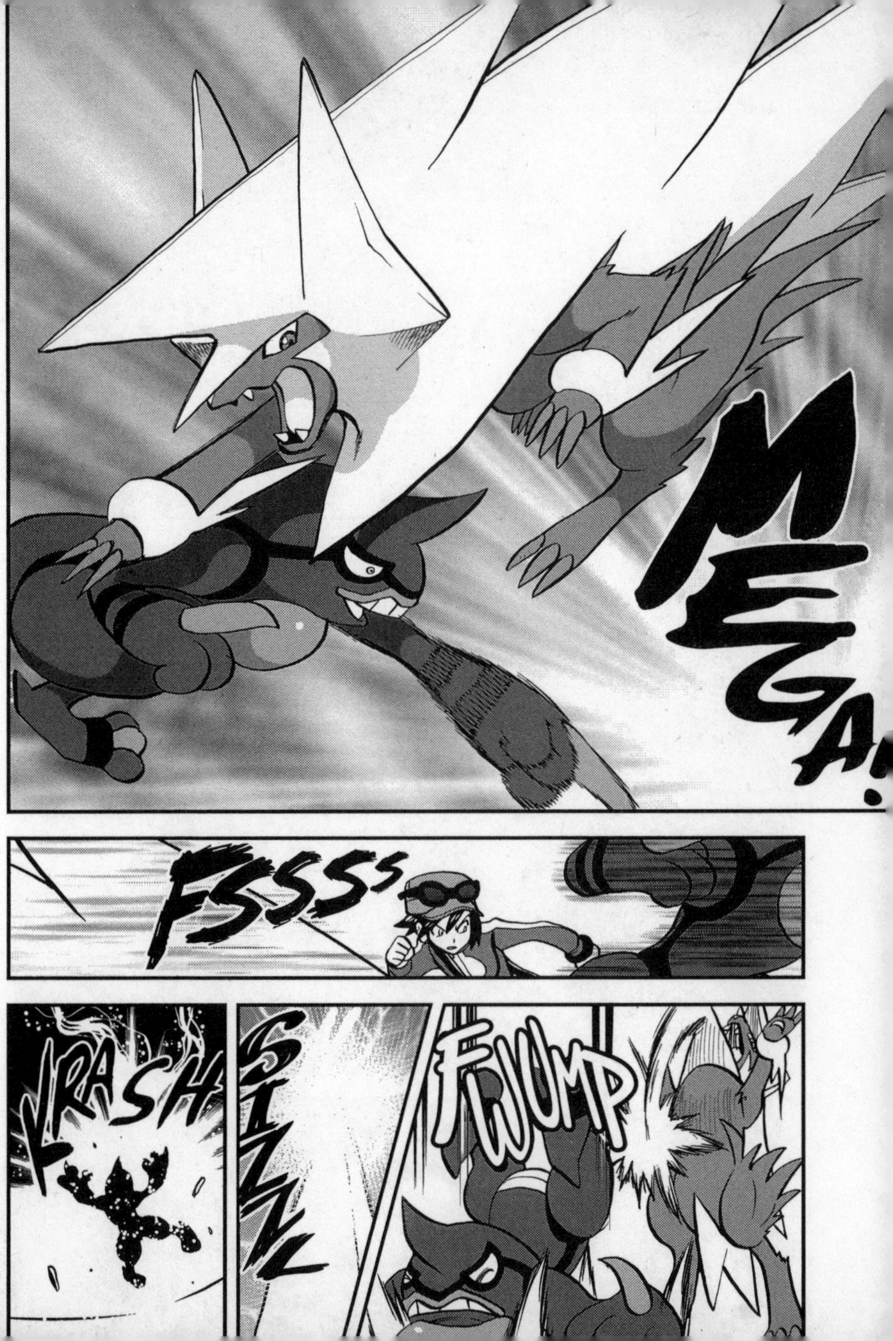
MEGA!
FSSSSS
FWUMP
SIZZZ
KRASH

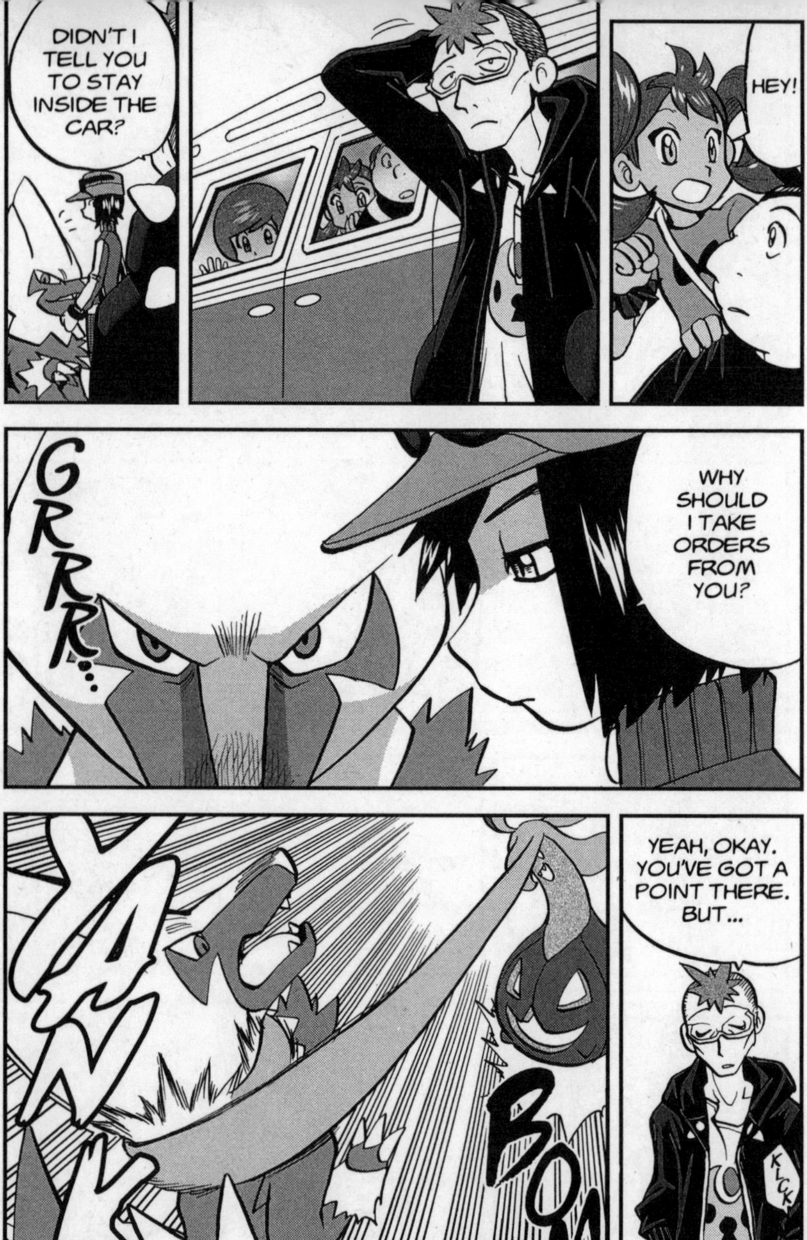
HEY!
DIDN'T I TELL YOU TO STAY INSIDE THE CAR?
WHY SHOULD I TAKE ORDERS FROM YOU?
GRRR...
YEAH, OKAY. YOU'VE GOT A POINT THERE. BUT...
KLICK
BOM

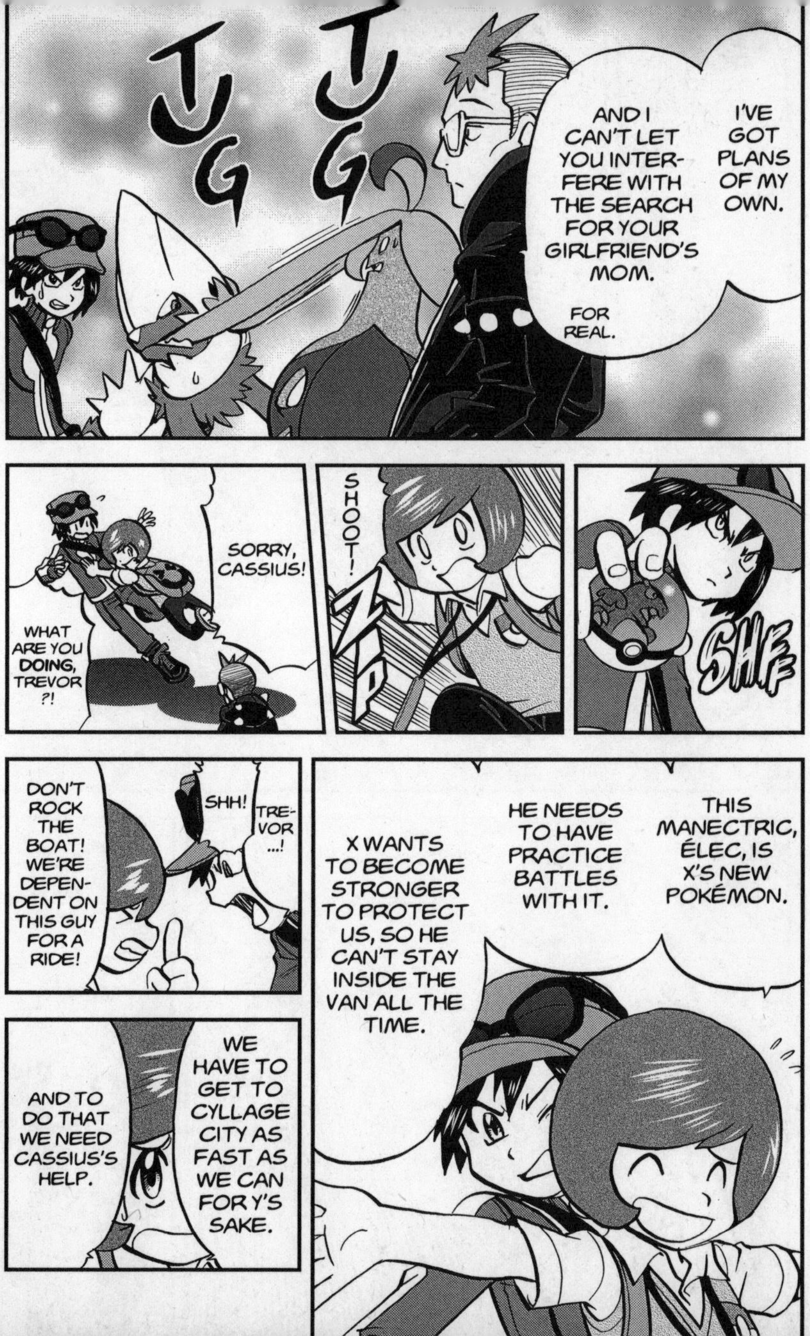

I'VE GOT PLANS OF MY OWN.
AND I CAN'T LET YOU INTER-FERE WITH THE SEARCH FOR YOUR GIRLFRIEND'S MOM.
FOR REAL.
TUG
TUG
SHFF
SHOOT!
ZIP
SORRY, CASSIUS!
WHAT ARE YOU DOING, TREVOR?!
THIS MANECTRIC, ÉLEC, IS X'S NEW POKÉMON.
HE NEEDS TO HAVE PRACTICE BATTLES WITH IT.
X WANTS TO BECOME STRONGER TO PROTECT US, SO HE CAN'T STAY INSIDE THE VAN ALL THE TIME.
TRE-VOR ...!
SHH!
DON'T ROCK THE BOAT! WE'RE DEPEN-DENT ON THIS GUY FOR A RIDE!
WE HAVE TO GET TO CYLLAGE CITY AS FAST AS WE CAN FOR Y'S SAKE.
AND TO DO THAT WE NEED CASSIUS'S HELP.

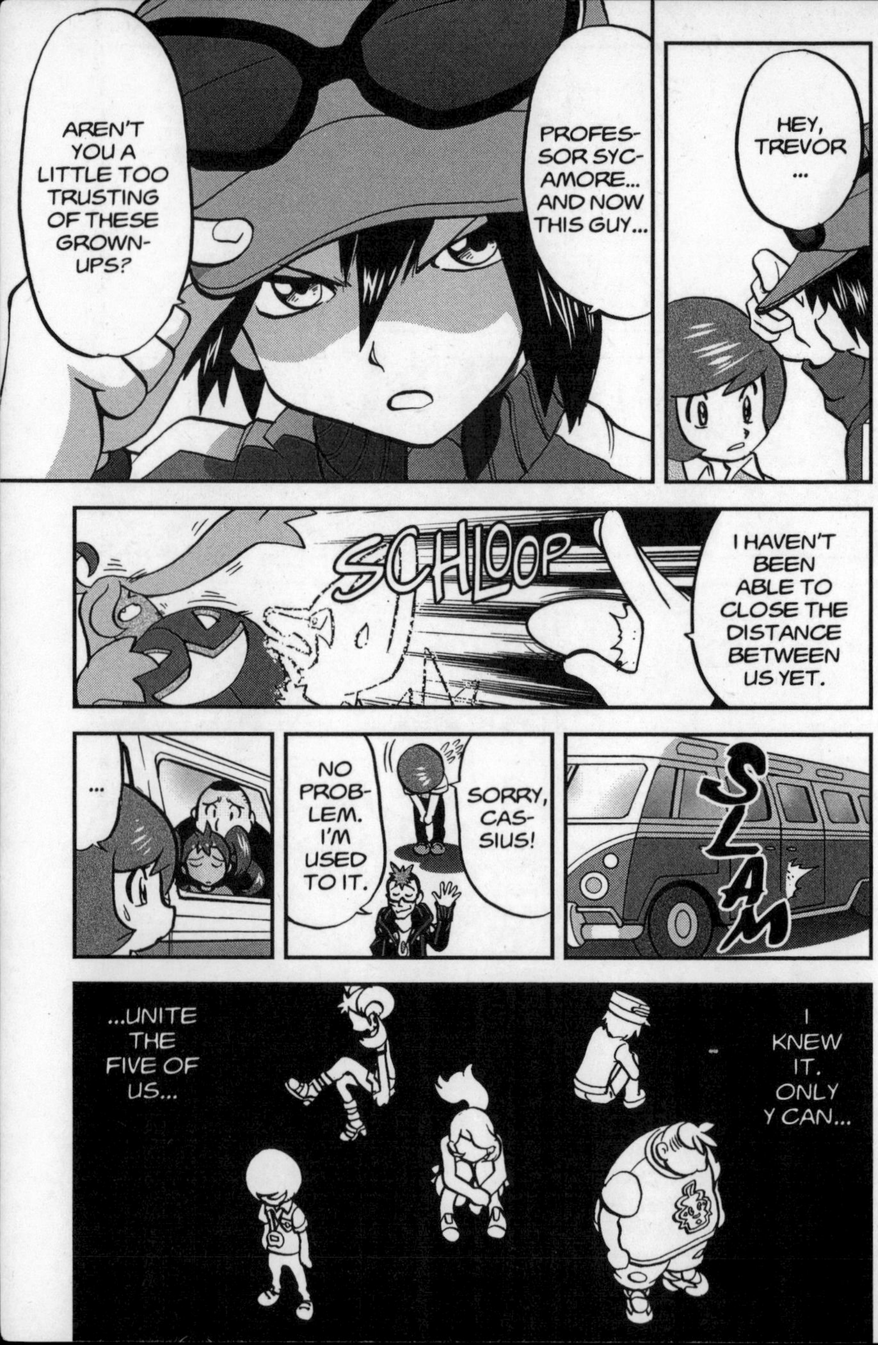
HEY, TREVOR ...
PROFESSOR SYCAMORE... AND NOW THIS GUY...
AREN'T YOU A LITTLE TOO TRUSTING OF THESE GROWN-UPS?
I HAVEN'T BEEN ABLE TO CLOSE THE DISTANCE BETWEEN US YET.
SCHLOOP
SLAM
SORRY, CASSIUS!
NO PROBLEM. I'M USED TO IT.
...
I KNEW IT. ONLY Y CAN...
...UNITE THE FIVE OF US...

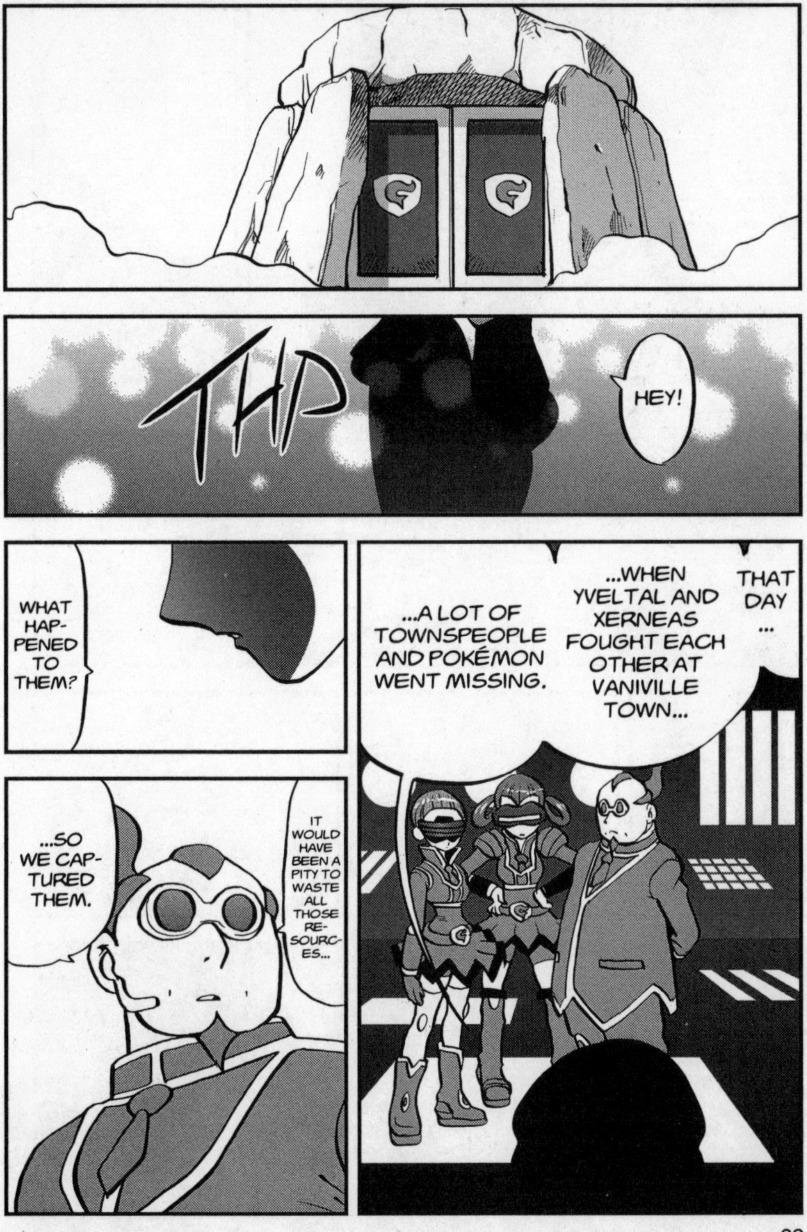
HEY!
THP
THAT DAY...
...WHEN YVELTAL AND XERNEAS FOUGHT EACH OTHER AT VANIVILLE TOWN...
...A LOT OF TOWNSPEOPLE AND POKÉMON WENT MISSING.
WHAT HAP-PENED TO THEM?
IT WOULD HAVE BEEN A PITY TO WASTE ALL THOSE RE-SOURC-ES...
...SO WE CAP-TURED THEM.

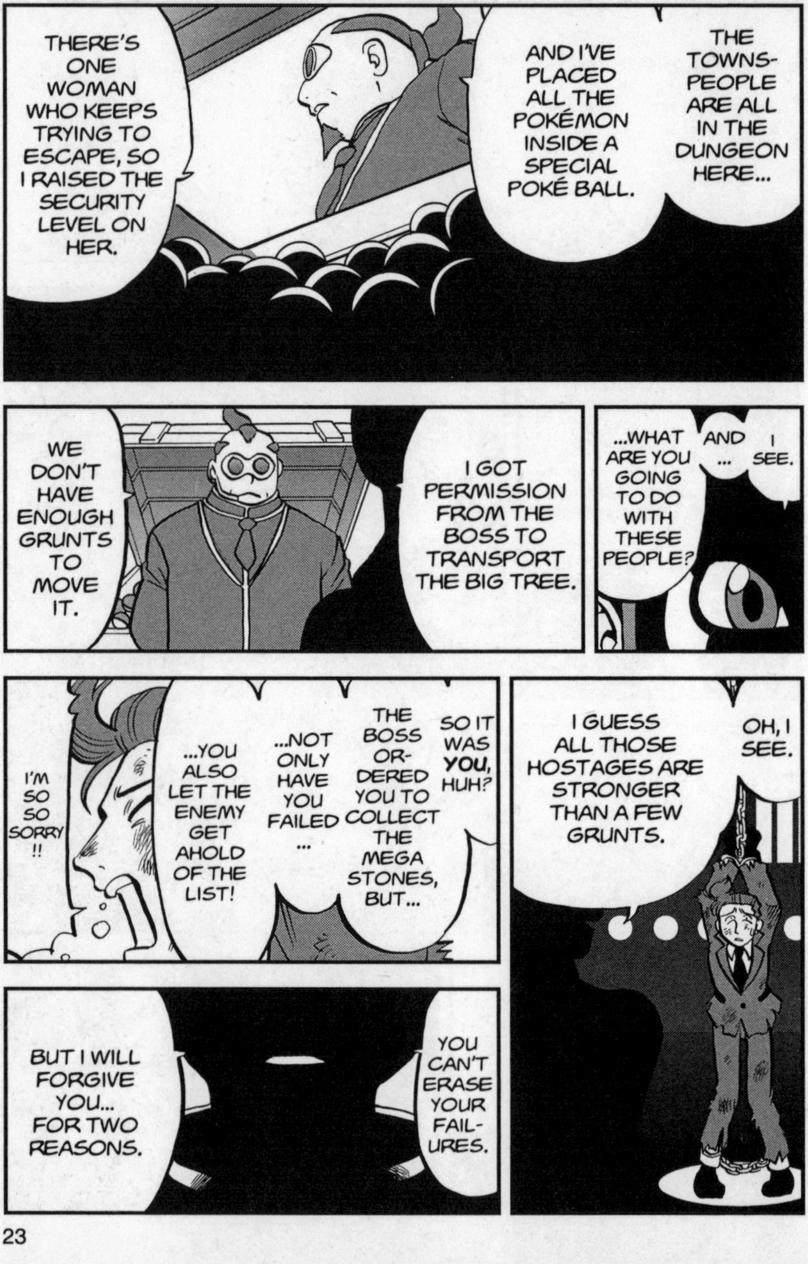
THE TOWNSPEOPLE ARE ALL IN THE DUNGEON HERE...
AND I'VE PLACED ALL THE POKÉMON INSIDE A SPECIAL POKÉ BALL.
THERE'S ONE WOMAN WHO KEEPS TRYING TO ESCAPE, SO I RAISED THE SECURITY LEVEL ON HER.
I SEE.
AND ...
...WHAT ARE YOU GOING TO DO WITH THESE PEOPLE?
I GOT PERMISSION FROM THE BOSS TO TRANSPORT THE BIG TREE.
WE DON'T HAVE ENOUGH GRUNTS TO MOVE IT.
OH, I SEE.
I GUESS ALL THOSE HOSTAGES ARE STRONGER THAN A FEW GRUNTS.
SO IT WAS **YOU**, HUH?
THE BOSS ORDERED YOU TO COLLECT THE MEGA STONES, BUT...
...NOT ONLY HAVE YOU FAILED...
...YOU ALSO LET THE ENEMY GET AHOLD OF THE LIST!
I'M SO SO SORRY!!
YOU CAN'T ERASE YOUR FAILURES.
BUT I WILL FORGIVE YOU... FOR TWO REASONS.

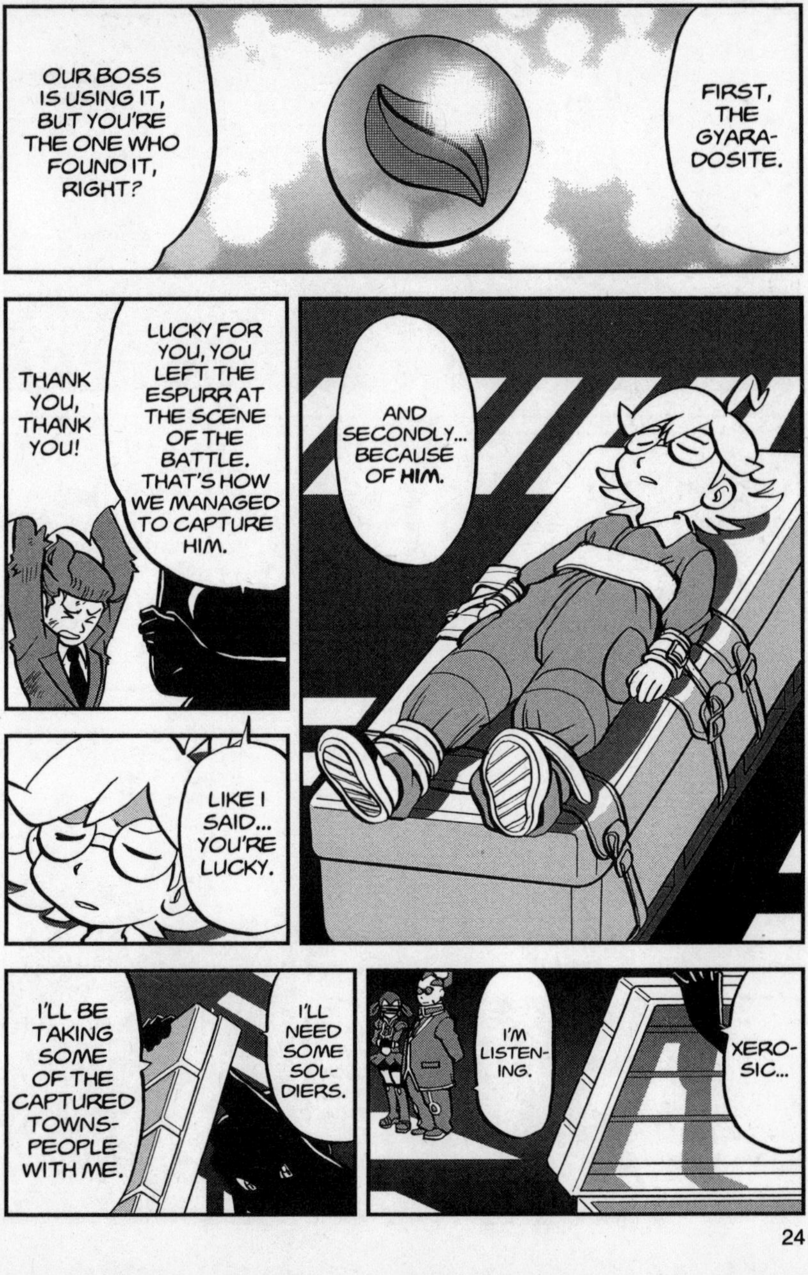
FIRST, THE GYARA-DOSITE.
OUR BOSS IS USING IT, BUT YOU'RE THE ONE WHO FOUND IT, RIGHT?
AND SECONDLY... BECAUSE OF **HIM**.
LUCKY FOR YOU, YOU LEFT THE ESPURR AT THE SCENE OF THE BATTLE. THAT'S HOW WE MANAGED TO CAPTURE HIM.
THANK YOU, THANK YOU!
LIKE I SAID... YOU'RE LUCKY.
XERO-SIC...
I'M LISTEN-ING.
I'LL NEED SOME SOL-DIERS.
I'LL BE TAKING SOME OF THE CAPTURED TOWNS-PEOPLE WITH ME.

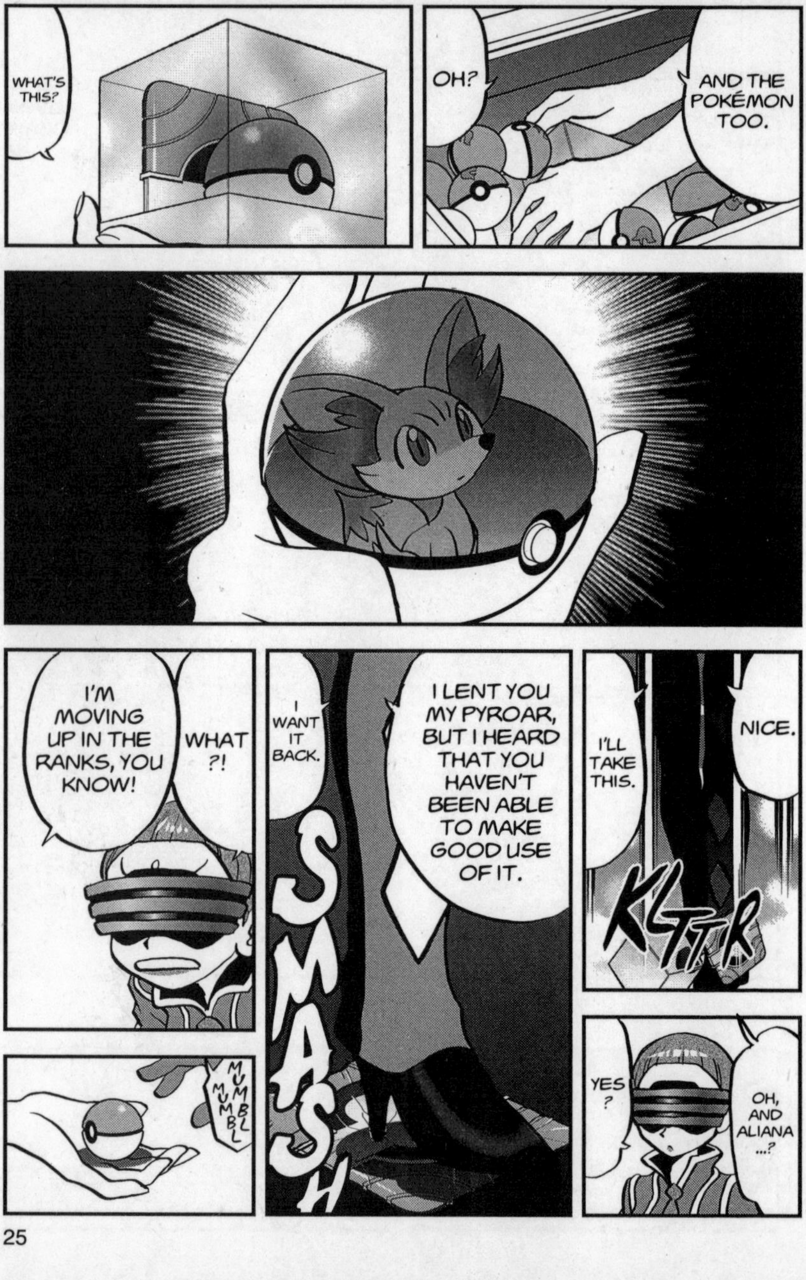
AND THE POKÉMON TOO.
OH?
WHAT'S THIS?
NICE.
I'LL TAKE THIS.
KLTTR
OH, AND ALIANA...?
YES?
I LENT YOU MY PYROAR, BUT I HEARD THAT YOU HAVEN'T BEEN ABLE TO MAKE GOOD USE OF IT.
I WANT IT BACK.
SMASH
WHAT?!
I'M MOVING UP IN THE RANKS, YOU KNOW!
MUMBL MUMBL

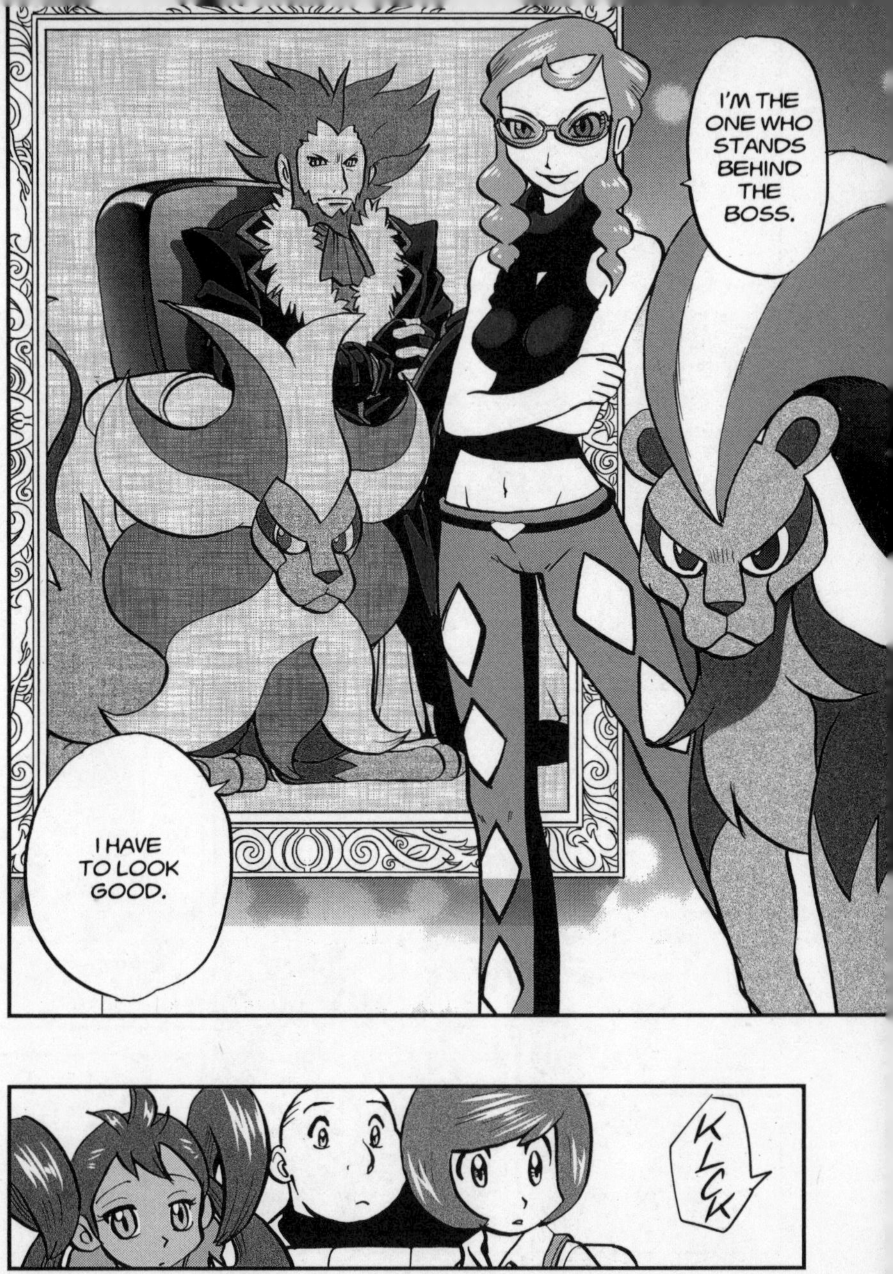
I'M THE ONE WHO STANDS BEHIND THE BOSS.
I HAVE TO LOOK GOOD.
KLICK

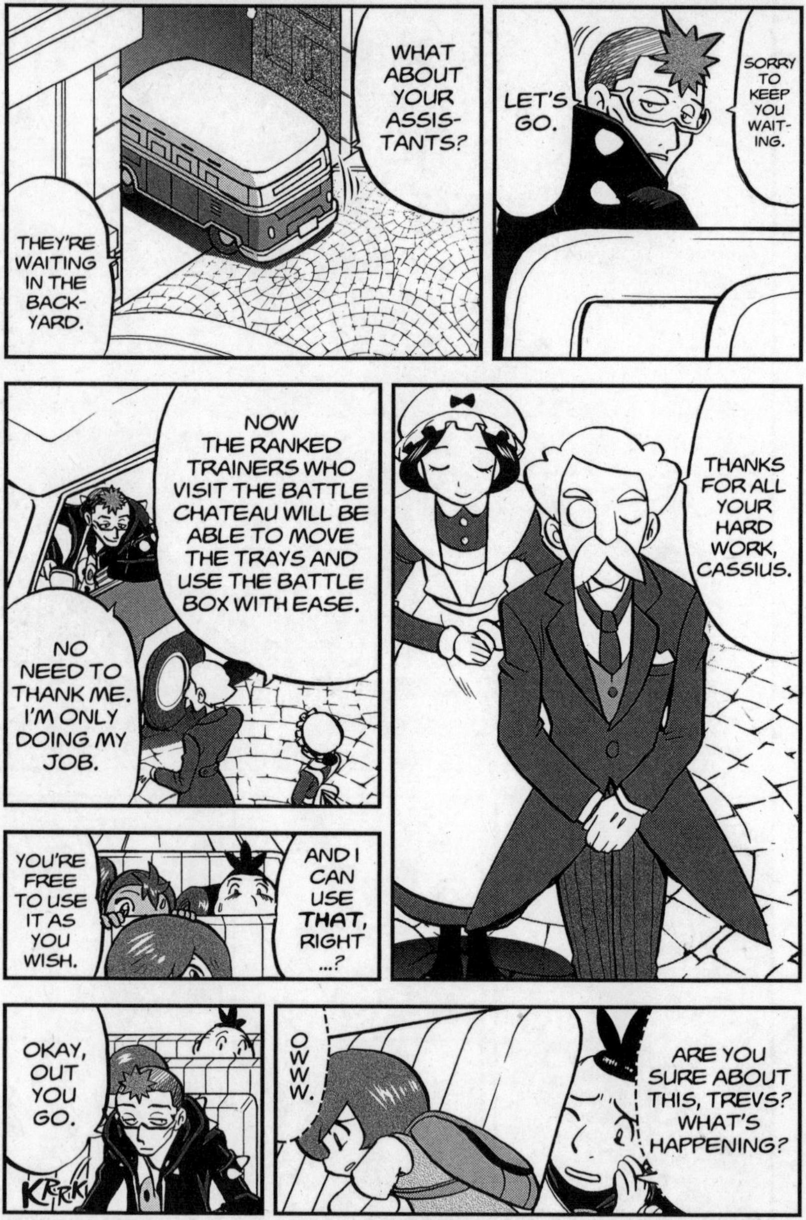
SORRY TO KEEP YOU WAITING.
LET'S GO.
WHAT ABOUT YOUR ASSISTANTS?
THEY'RE WAITING IN THE BACKYARD.
THANKS FOR ALL YOUR HARD WORK, CASSIUS.
NOW THE RANKED TRAINERS WHO VISIT THE BATTLE CHATEAU WILL BE ABLE TO MOVE THE TRAYS AND USE THE BATTLE BOX WITH EASE.
NO NEED TO THANK ME. I'M ONLY DOING MY JOB.
AND I CAN USE **THAT**, RIGHT ...?
YOU'RE FREE TO USE IT AS YOU WISH.
ARE YOU SURE ABOUT THIS, TREVS? WHAT'S HAPPENING?
OWWW.
OKAY, OUT YOU GO.
KRRRK

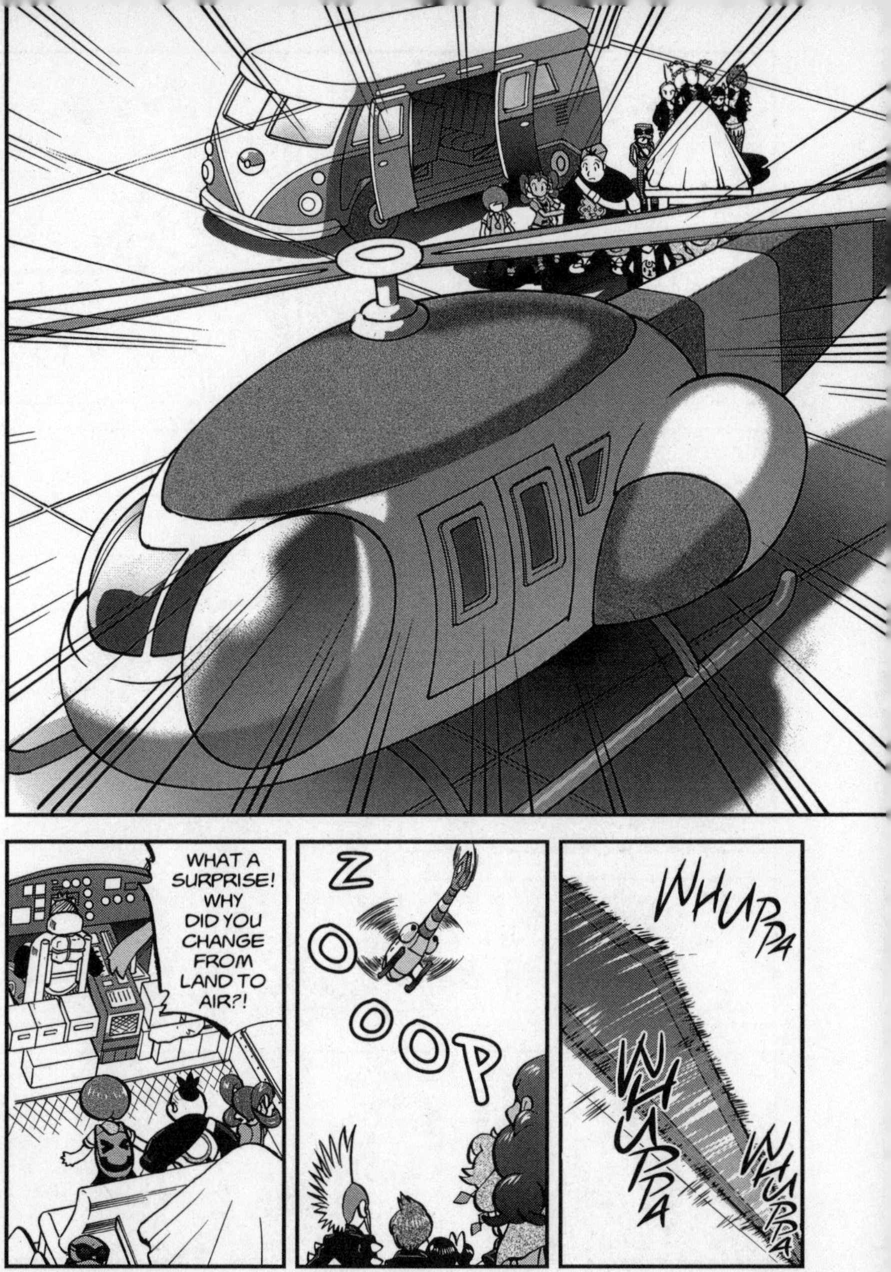
WHUPPA
WHUPPA
WHUPPA
WHUPPA
ZOOOP
WHAT A SURPRISE! WHY DID YOU CHANGE FROM LAND TO AIR?!

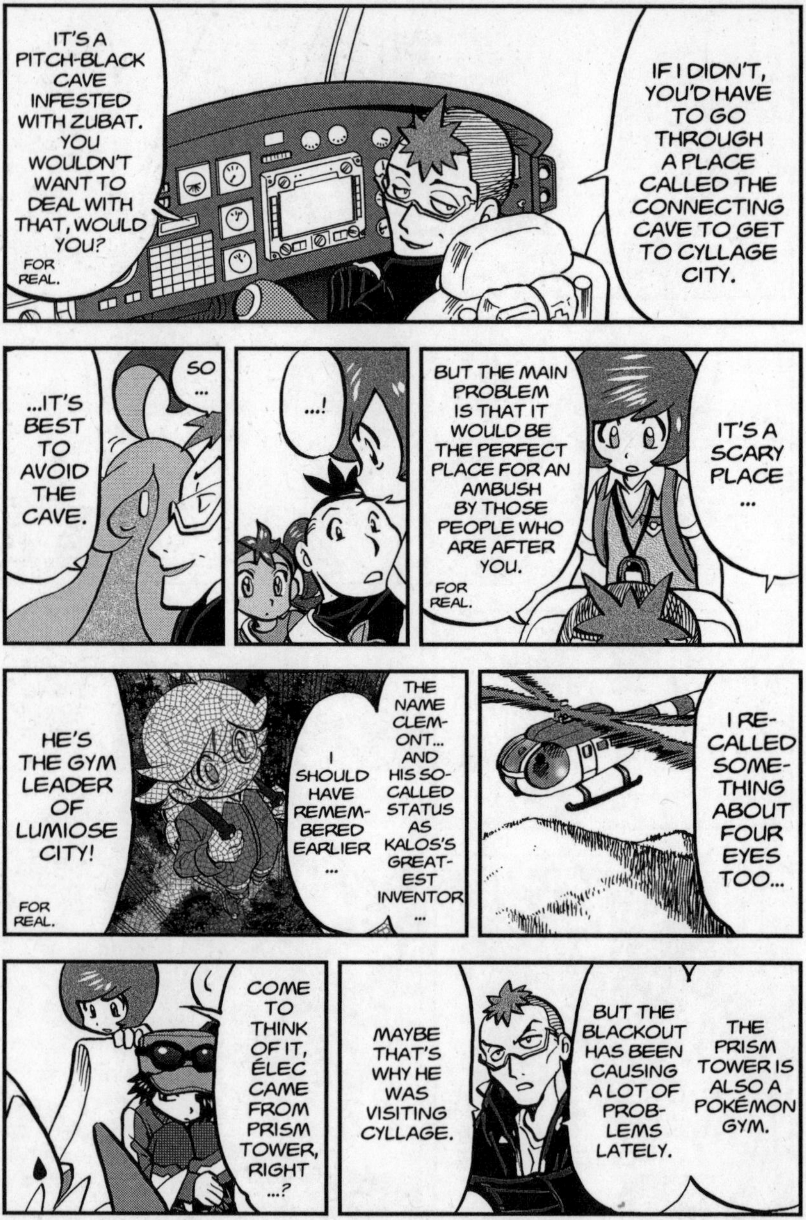
IF I DIDN'T, YOU'D HAVE TO GO THROUGH A PLACE CALLED THE CONNECTING CAVE TO GET TO CYLLAGE CITY.
IT'S A PITCH-BLACK CAVE INFESTED WITH ZUBAT. YOU WOULDN'T WANT TO DEAL WITH THAT, WOULD YOU?
FOR REAL.
IT'S A SCARY PLACE ...
BUT THE MAIN PROBLEM IS THAT IT WOULD BE THE PERFECT PLACE FOR AN AMBUSH BY THOSE PEOPLE WHO ARE AFTER YOU.
FOR REAL.
...!
SO ...
...IT'S BEST TO AVOID THE CAVE.
I RECALLED SOMETHING ABOUT FOUR EYES TOO...
THE NAME CLEMONT... AND HIS SO-CALLED STATUS AS KALOS'S GREATEST INVENTOR ...
I SHOULD HAVE REMEMBERED EARLIER ...
HE'S THE GYM LEADER OF LUMIOSE CITY!
FOR REAL.
THE PRISM TOWER IS ALSO A POKÉMON GYM.
BUT THE BLACKOUT HAS BEEN CAUSING A LOT OF PROBLEMS LATELY.
MAYBE THAT'S WHY HE WAS VISITING CYLLAGE.
COME TO THINK OF IT, ÉLEC CAME FROM PRISM TOWER, RIGHT ...?

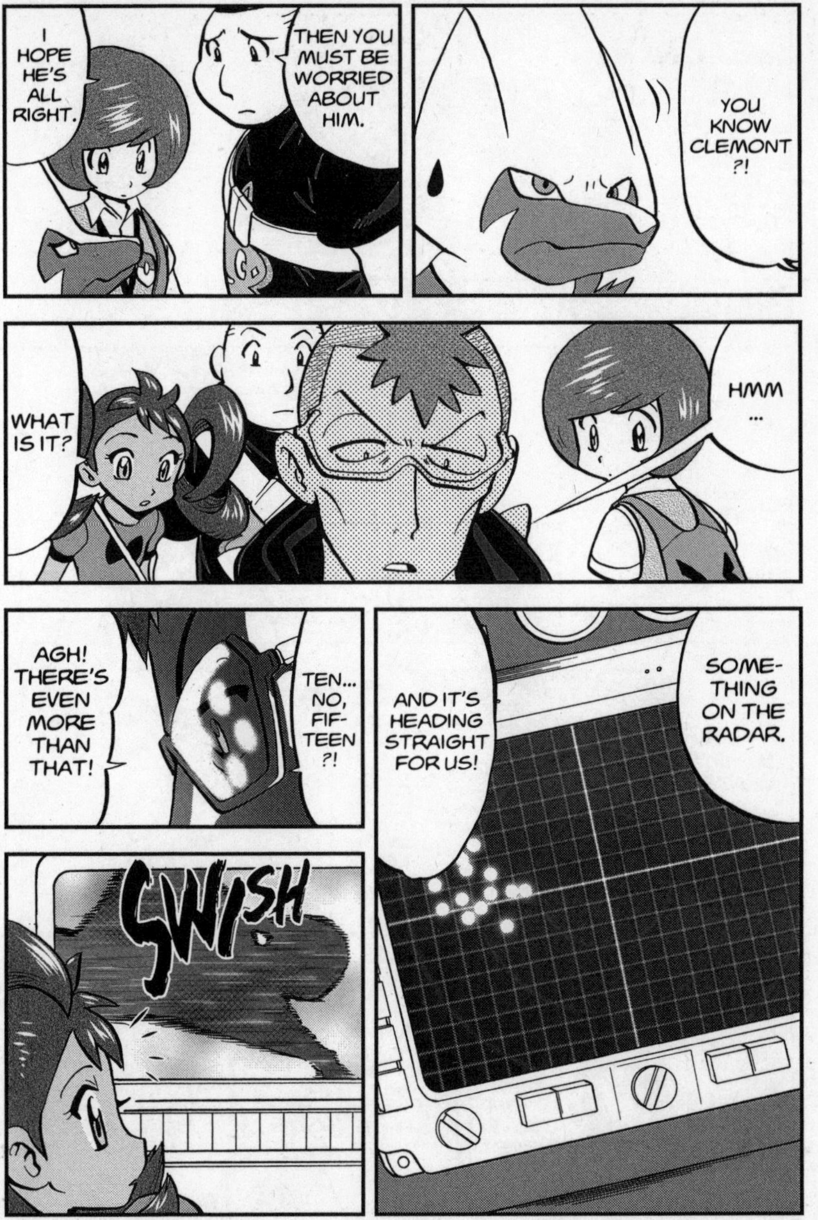
YOU KNOW CLEMONT ?!
THEN YOU MUST BE WORRIED ABOUT HIM.
I HOPE HE'S ALL RIGHT.
HMM ...
WHAT IS IT?
SOME-THING ON THE RADAR.
AND IT'S HEADING STRAIGHT FOR US!
TEN... NO, FIF-TEEN ?!
AGH! THERE'S EVEN MORE THAN THAT!
SWISH

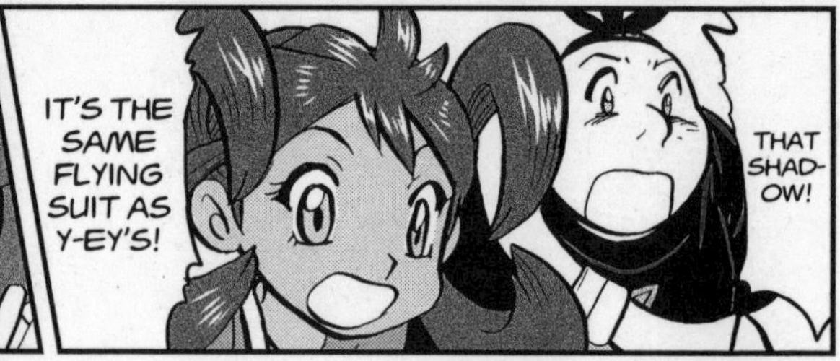
THAT SHADOW!
IT'S THE SAME FLYING SUIT AS Y-EY'S!

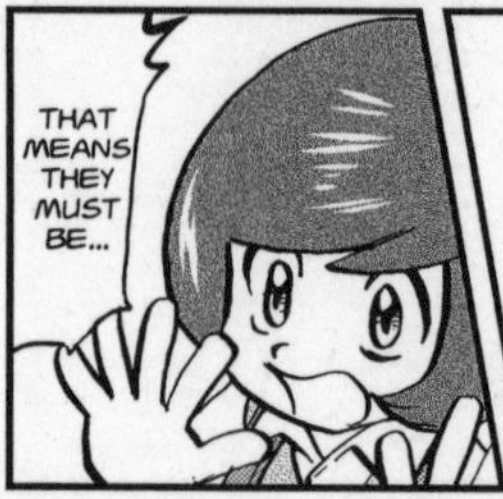
THAT MEANS THEY MUST BE...

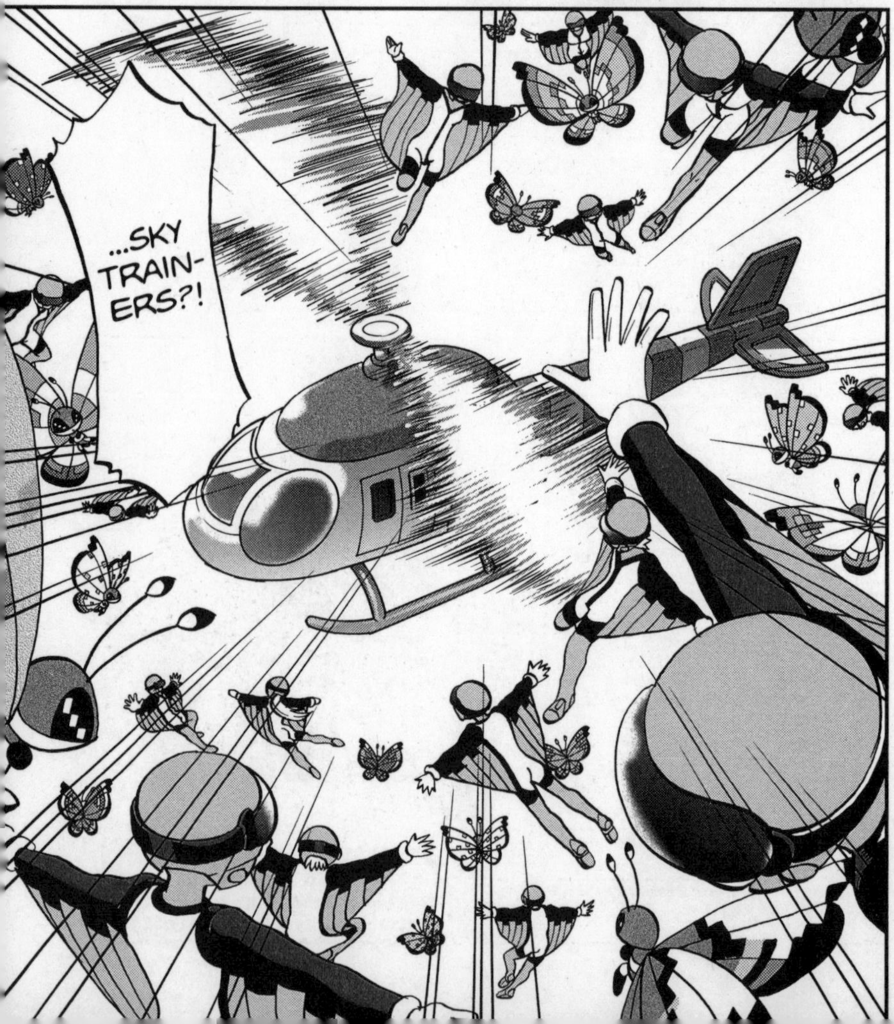
...SKY TRAINERS?!

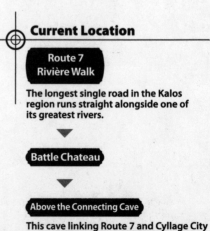

Current Location

Route 7
Rivière Walk

The longest single road in the Kalos region runs straight alongside one of its greatest rivers.

▼

Battle Chateau

▼

Above the Connecting Cave

This cave linking Route 7 and Cyllage City is notable for its great hordes of Zubat.
* They used an air route to avoid the cave.

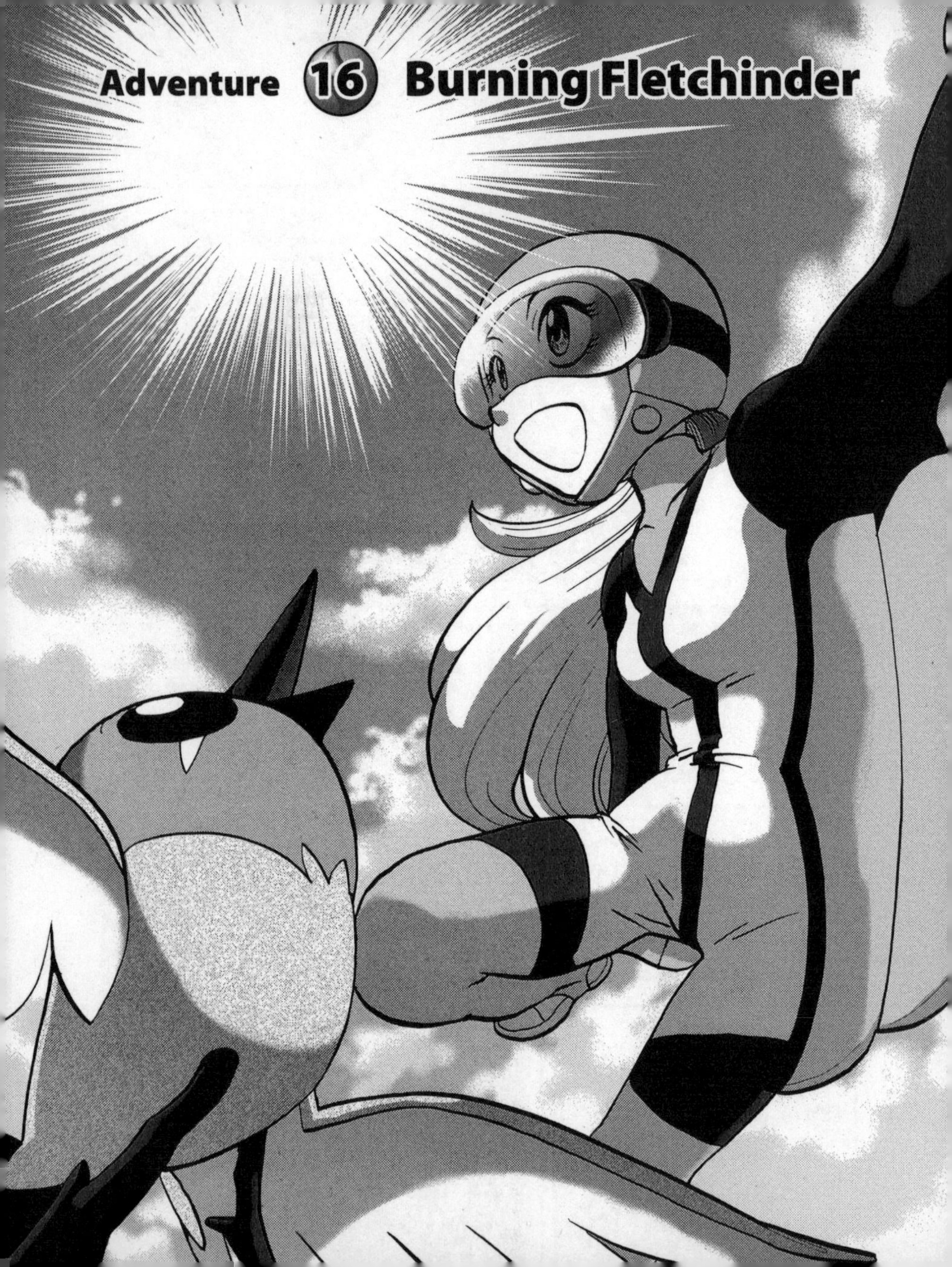
Adventure 16 Burning Fletchinder

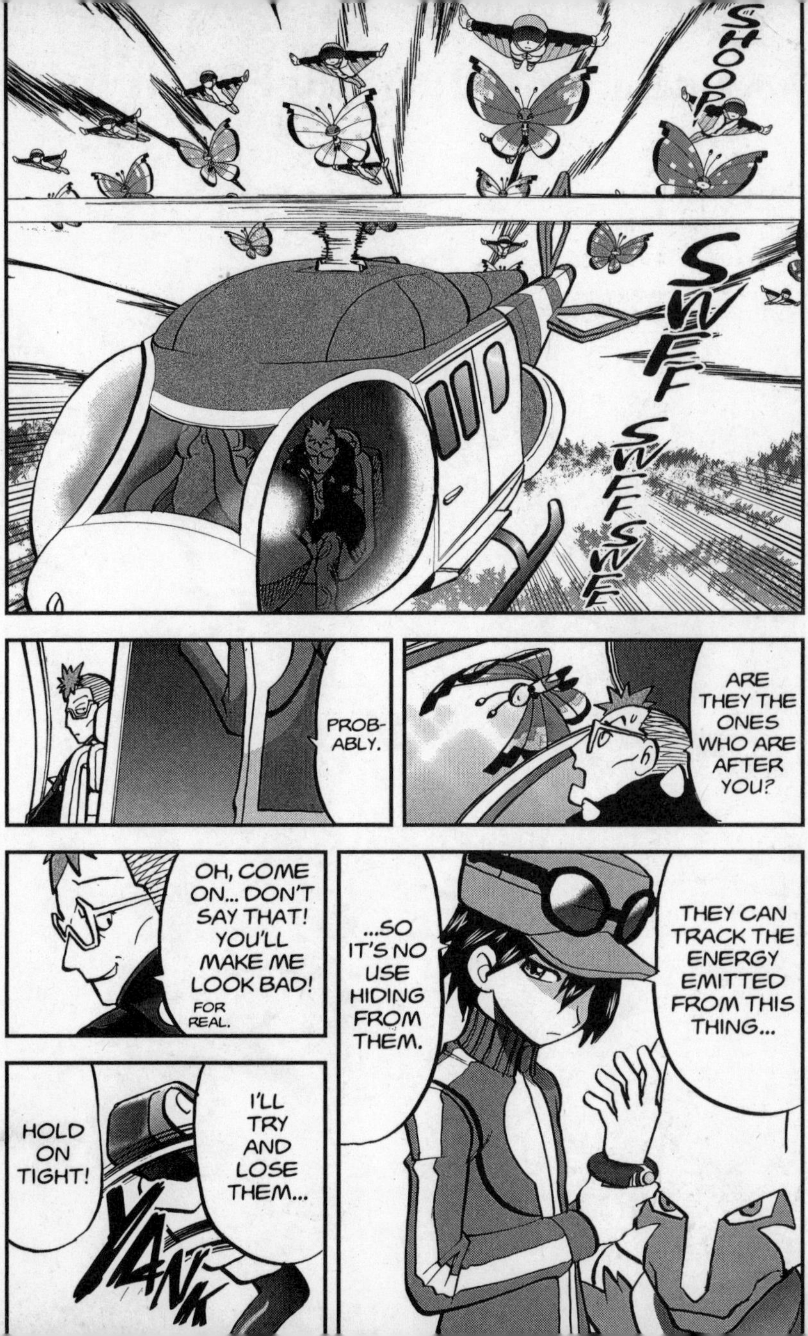
SHOOOP
SWFF
SWFFSWF
ARE THEY THE ONES WHO ARE AFTER YOU?
PROB-ABLY.
THEY CAN TRACK THE ENERGY EMITTED FROM THIS THING...
...SO IT'S NO USE HIDING FROM THEM.
OH, COME ON... DON'T SAY THAT! YOU'LL MAKE ME LOOK BAD!
FOR REAL.
I'LL TRY AND LOSE THEM...
HOLD ON TIGHT!
YANK

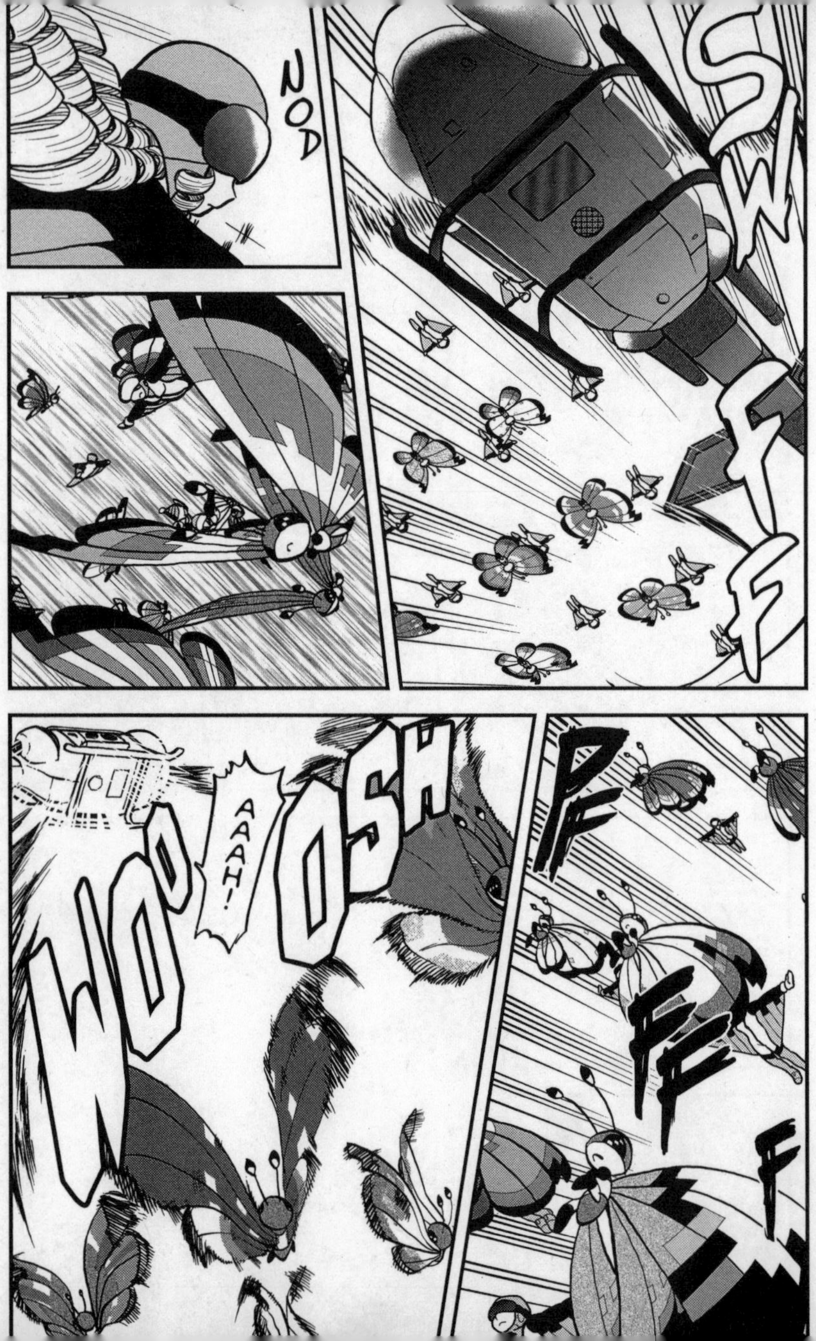
SWFF
NOD
PFFF
AAAH!
WOOOSH

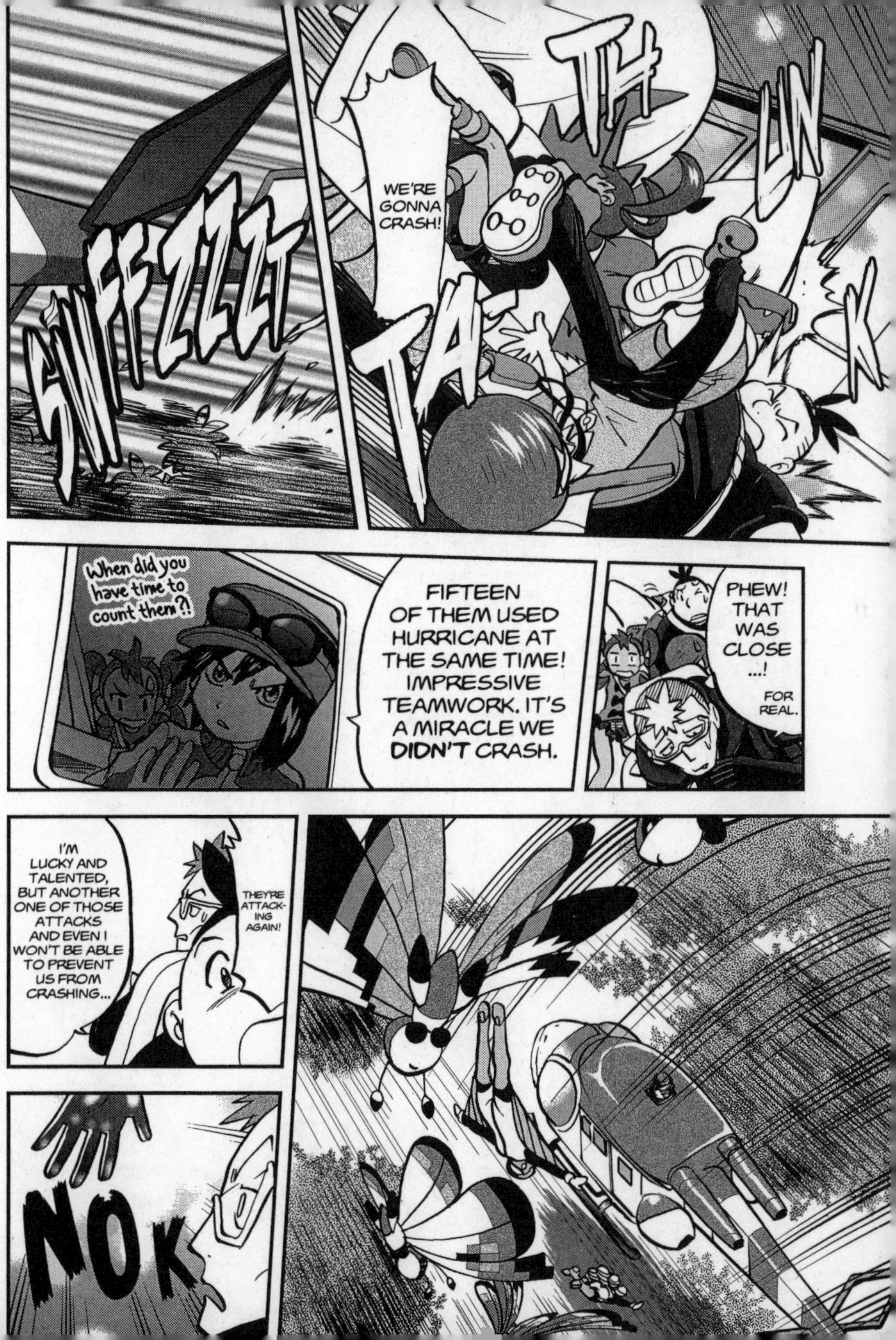
THUNK
WE'RE GONNA CRASH!
TA
SHFFZZZT
PHEW! THAT WAS CLOSE ...!
FOR REAL.
FIFTEEN OF THEM USED HURRICANE AT THE SAME TIME! IMPRESSIVE TEAMWORK. IT'S A MIRACLE WE **DIDN'T** CRASH.
When did you have time to count them?!
THEY'RE ATTACK-ING AGAIN!
I'M LUCKY AND TALENTED, BUT ANOTHER ONE OF THOSE ATTACKS AND EVEN I WON'T BE ABLE TO PREVENT US FROM CRASHING...
NOK

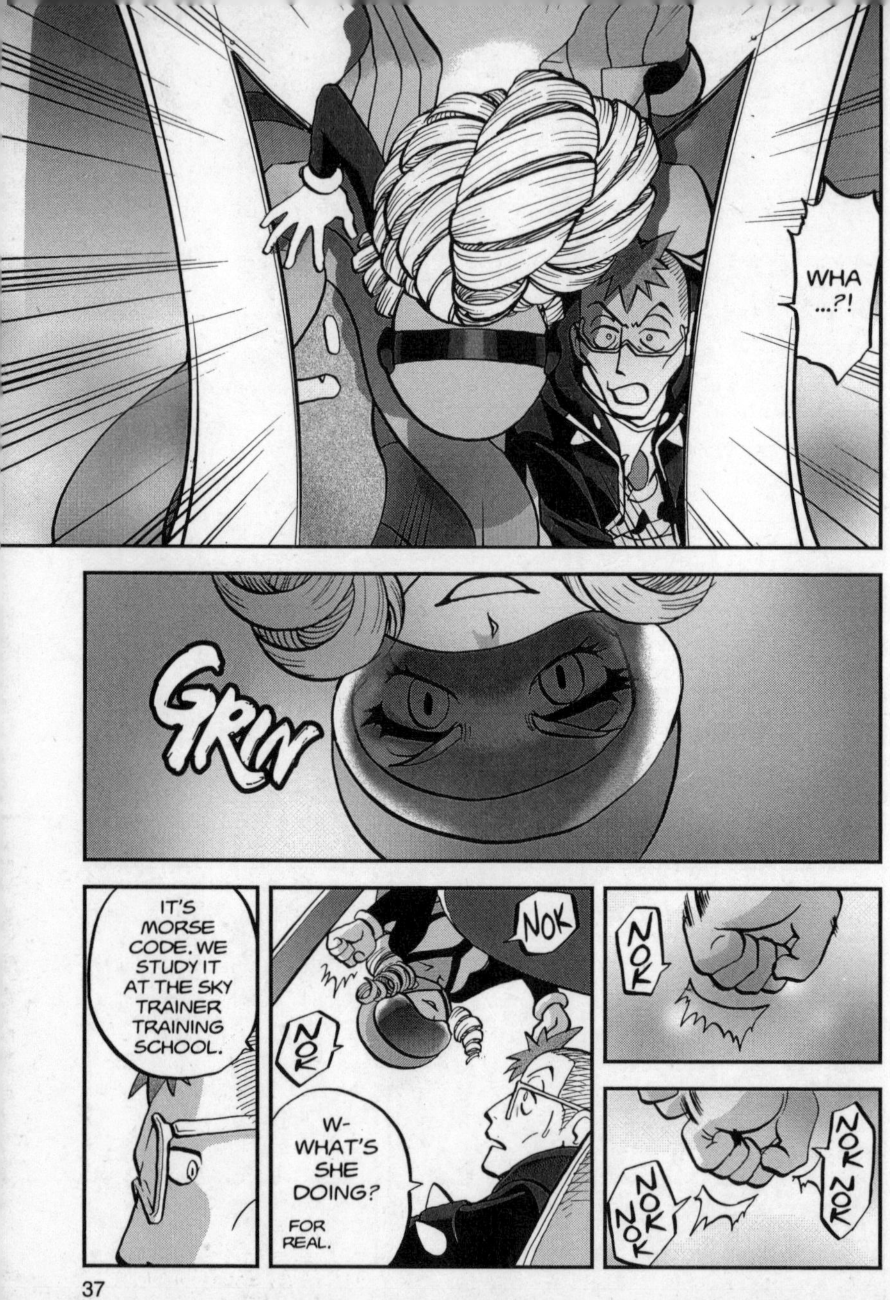

WHA ...?!
GRIN
NOK NOK
NOK NOK
NOK NOK
NOK
NOK
W- WHAT'S SHE DOING?
FOR REAL.
IT'S MORSE CODE. WE STUDY IT AT THE SKY TRAINER TRAINING SCHOOL.

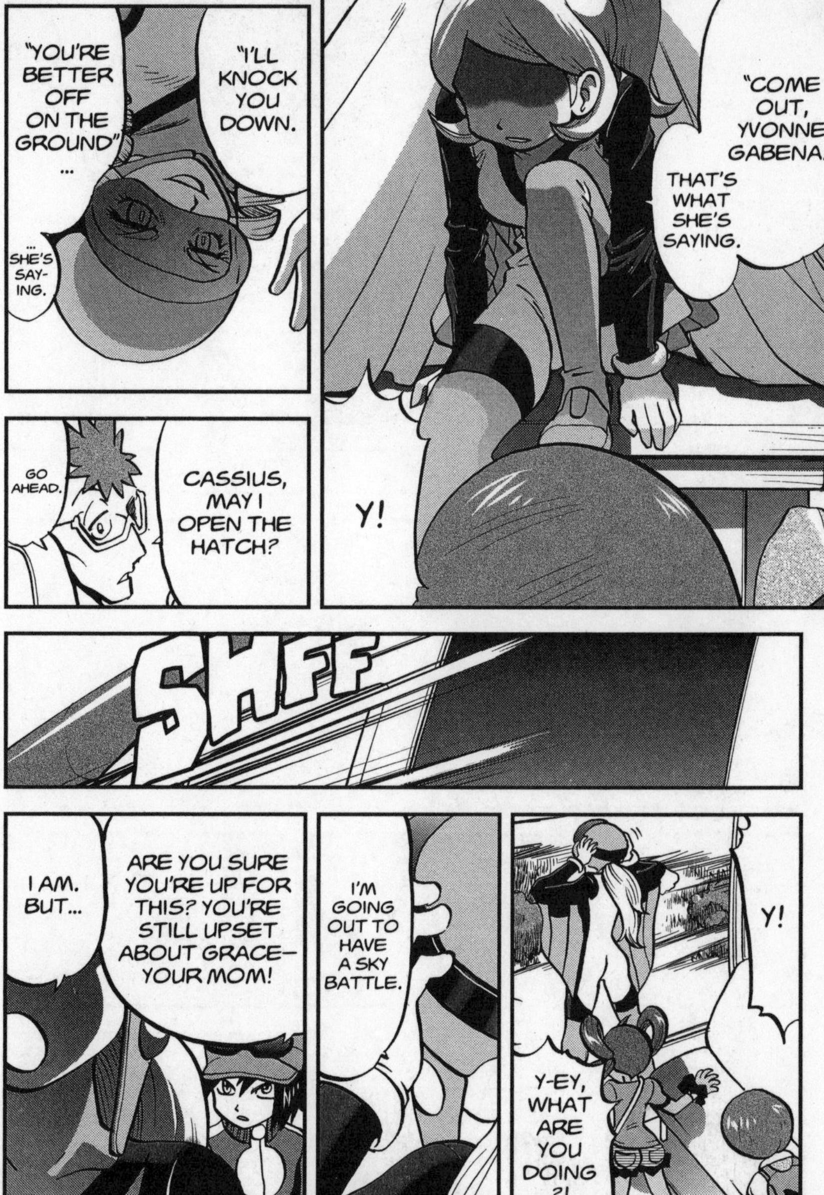
"COME OUT, YVONNE GABENA."
THAT'S WHAT SHE'S SAYING.
Y!
"I'LL KNOCK YOU DOWN.
"YOU'RE BETTER OFF ON THE GROUND" ...
... SHE'S SAY-ING.
CASSIUS, MAY I OPEN THE HATCH?
GO AHEAD.
SHFF
Y!
Y-EY, WHAT ARE YOU DOING ?!
I'M GOING OUT TO HAVE A SKY BATTLE.
ARE YOU SURE YOU'RE UP FOR THIS? YOU'RE STILL UPSET ABOUT GRACE—YOUR MOM!
I AM. BUT...

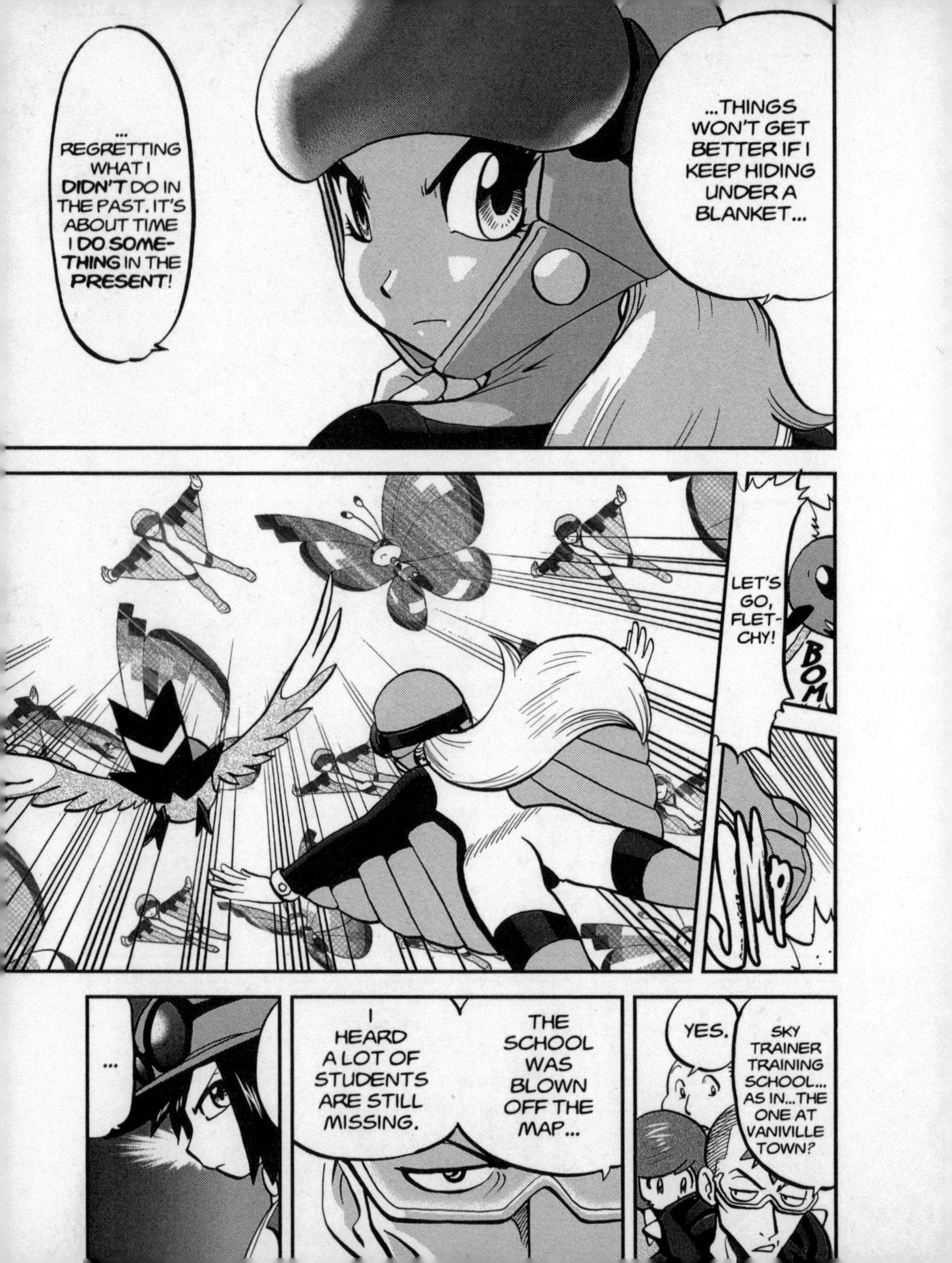
...THINGS WON'T GET BETTER IF I KEEP HIDING UNDER A BLANKET...
...REGRETTING WHAT I DIDN'T DO IN THE PAST. IT'S ABOUT TIME I DO SOMETHING IN THE PRESENT!
LET'S GO, FLETCHY!
BOM
SKY TRAINER TRAINING SCHOOL... AS IN...THE ONE AT VANIVILLE TOWN?
YES.
THE SCHOOL WAS BLOWN OFF THE MAP...
I HEARD A LOT OF STUDENTS ARE STILL MISSING.
...

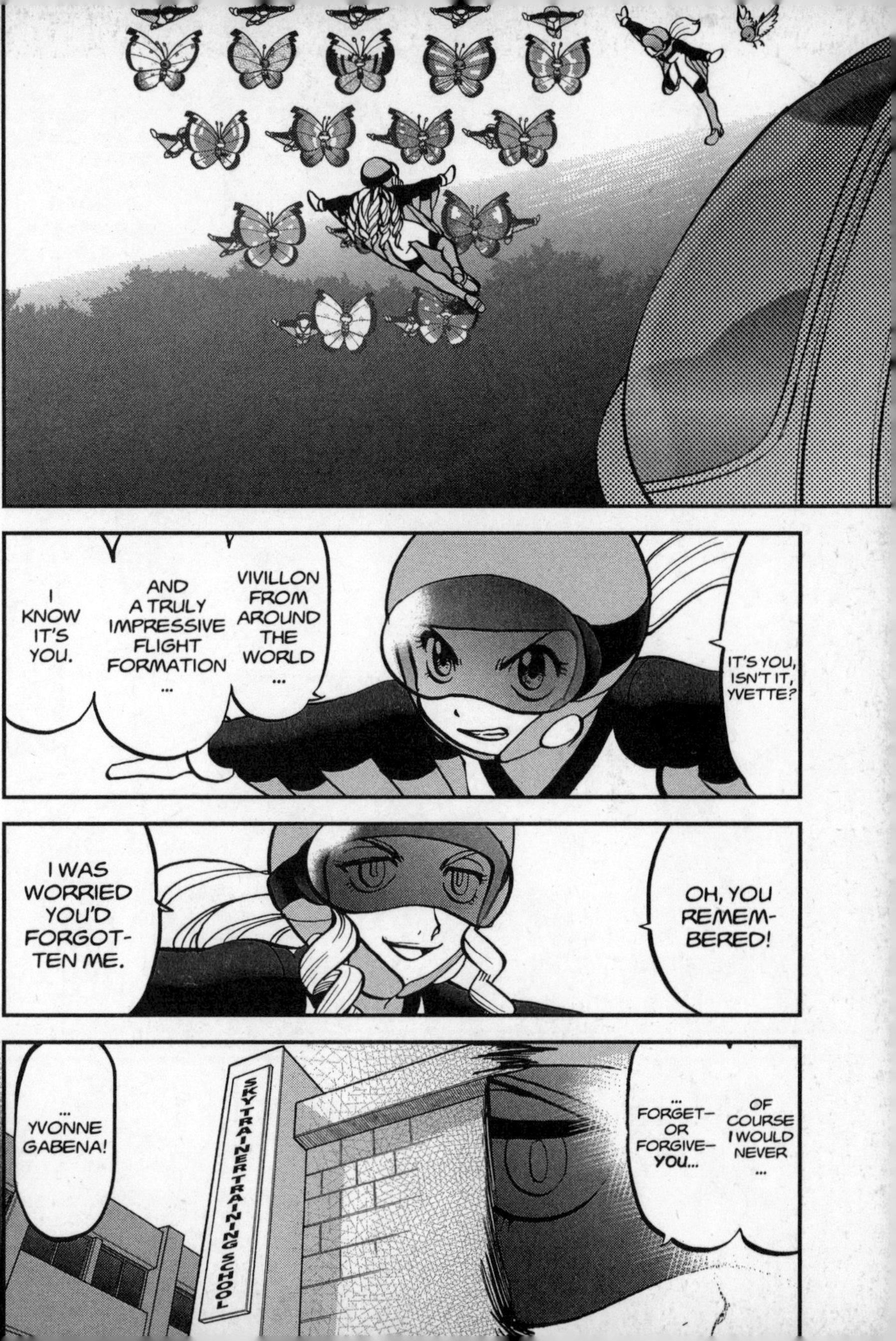
IT'S YOU, ISN'T IT, YVETTE?
VIVILLON FROM AROUND THE WORLD ...
AND A TRULY IMPRESSIVE FLIGHT FORMATION ...
I KNOW IT'S YOU.
OH, YOU REMEMBERED!
I WAS WORRIED YOU'D FORGOTTEN ME.
OF COURSE I WOULD NEVER ...
... FORGET—OR FORGIVE—**YOU**...
SKY TRAINER TRAINING SCHOOL
... YVONNE GABENA!

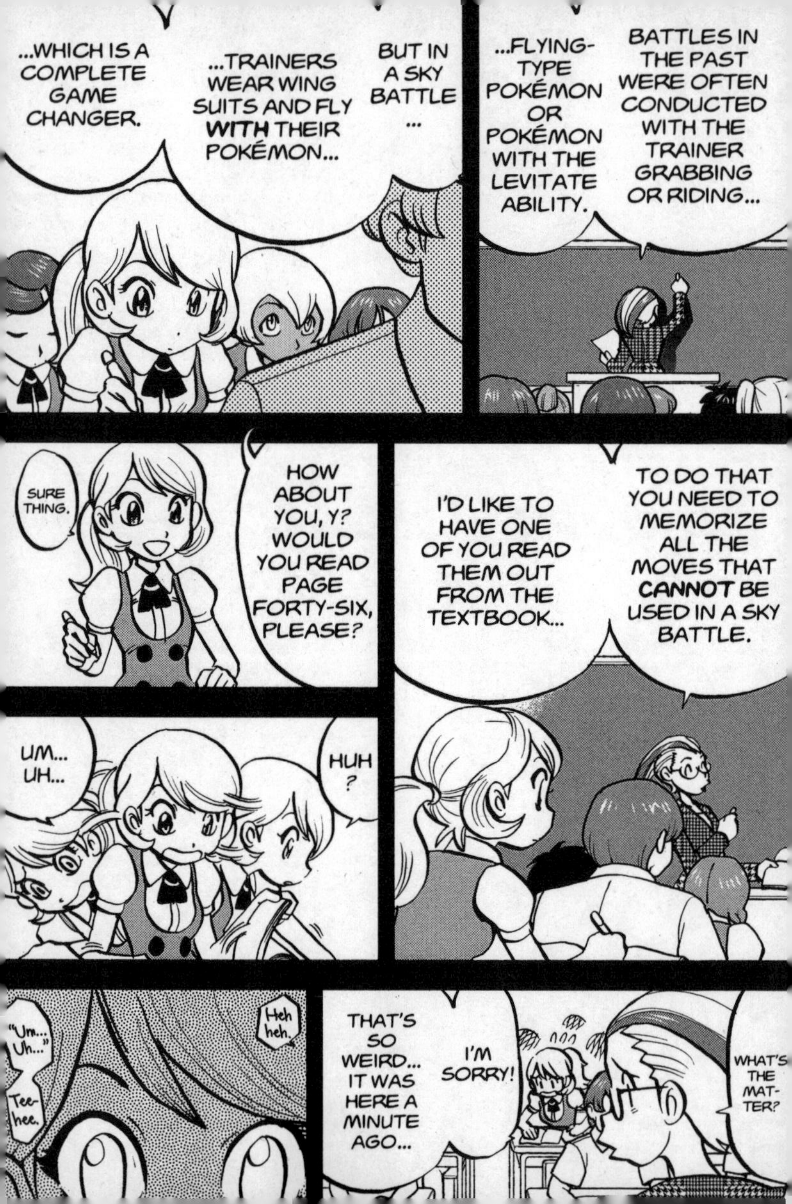
BATTLES IN THE PAST WERE OFTEN CONDUCTED WITH THE TRAINER GRABBING OR RIDING...
...FLYING-TYPE POKÉMON OR POKÉMON WITH THE LEVITATE ABILITY.
BUT IN A SKY BATTLE ...
...TRAINERS WEAR WING SUITS AND FLY **WITH** THEIR POKÉMON...
...WHICH IS A COMPLETE GAME CHANGER.
TO DO THAT YOU NEED TO MEMORIZE ALL THE MOVES THAT **CANNOT** BE USED IN A SKY BATTLE.
I'D LIKE TO HAVE ONE OF YOU READ THEM OUT FROM THE TEXTBOOK...
HOW ABOUT YOU, Y? WOULD YOU READ PAGE FORTY-SIX, PLEASE?
SURE THING.
HUH?
UM... UH...
WHAT'S THE MATTER?
I'M SORRY!
THAT'S SO WEIRD... IT WAS HERE A MINUTE AGO...
Heh heh.
"Um... Uh..."
Tee-hee.

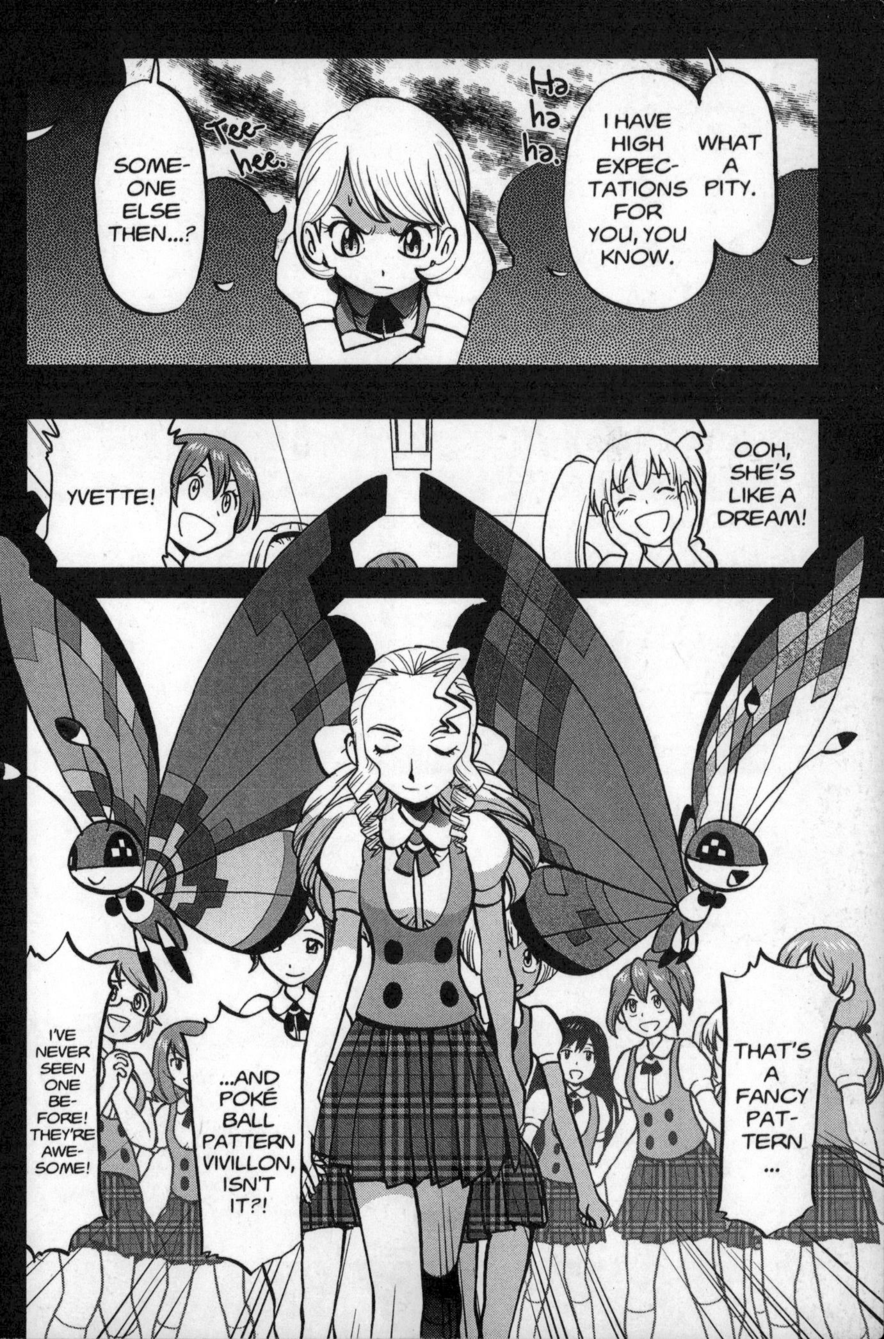
WHAT A PITY.
I HAVE HIGH EXPECTATIONS FOR YOU, YOU KNOW.
Ha ha ha.
Tee-hee.
SOME-ONE ELSE THEN...?
OOH, SHE'S LIKE A DREAM!
YVETTE!
THAT'S A FANCY PAT-TERN...
...AND POKÉ BALL PATTERN VIVILLON, ISN'T IT?!
I'VE NEVER SEEN ONE BE-FORE! THEY'RE AWE-SOME!

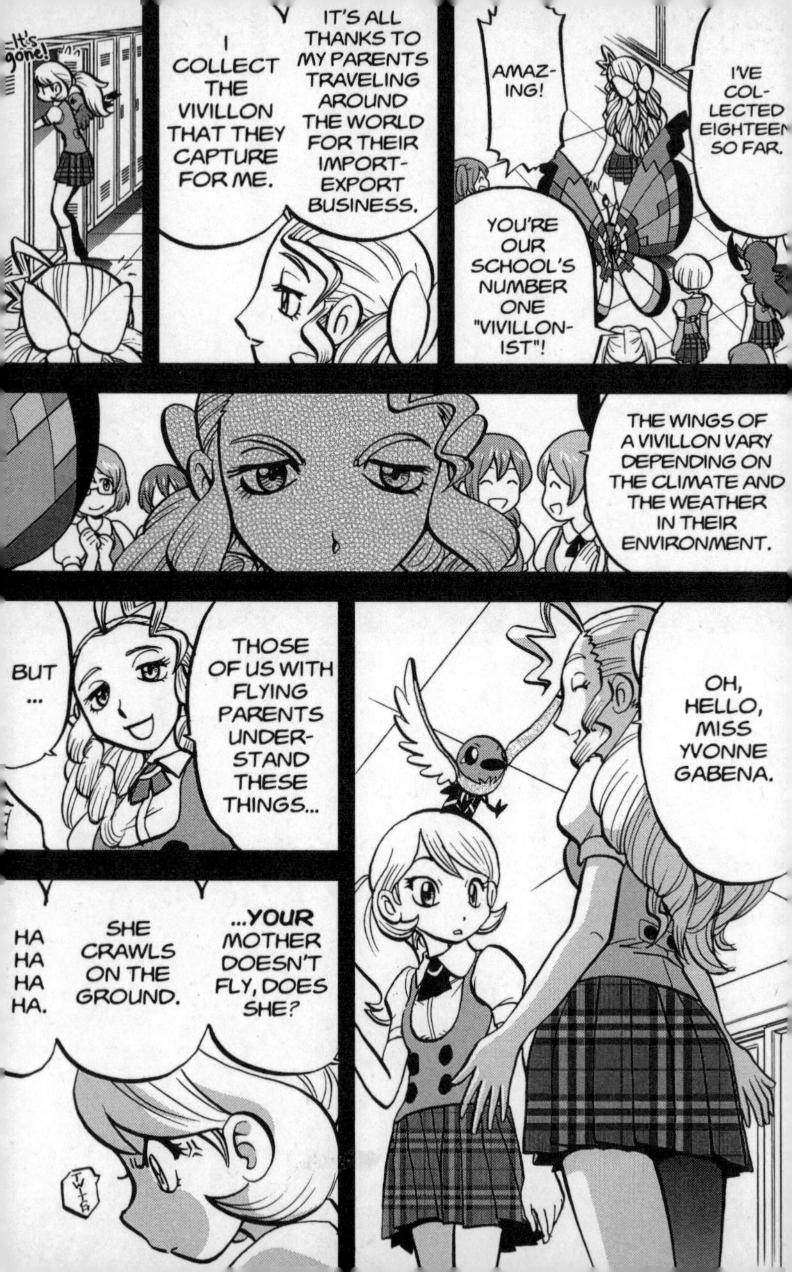
I'VE COLLECTED EIGHTEEN SO FAR.
AMAZING!
YOU'RE OUR SCHOOL'S NUMBER ONE "VIVILLONIST"!
IT'S ALL THANKS TO MY PARENTS TRAVELING AROUND THE WORLD FOR THEIR IMPORT-EXPORT BUSINESS.
I COLLECT THE VIVILLON THAT THEY CAPTURE FOR ME.
It's gone!
THE WINGS OF A VIVILLON VARY DEPENDING ON THE CLIMATE AND THE WEATHER IN THEIR ENVIRONMENT.
OH, HELLO, MISS YVONNE GABENA.
THOSE OF US WITH FLYING PARENTS UNDERSTAND THESE THINGS...
BUT ...
...YOUR MOTHER DOESN'T FLY, DOES SHE?
SHE CRAWLS ON THE GROUND.
HA HA HA HA.
TWITCH

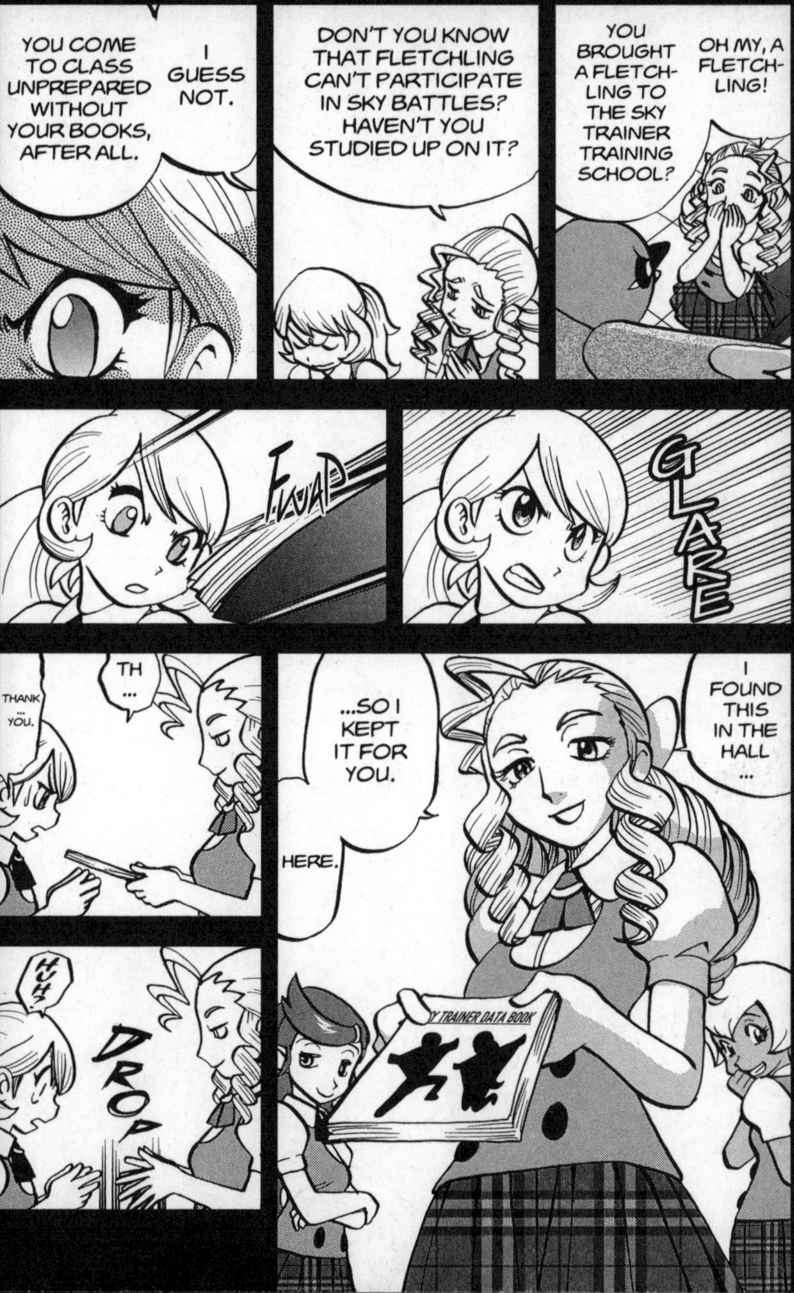
OH MY, A FLETCH-LING!
YOU BROUGHT A FLETCH-LING TO THE SKY TRAINER TRAINING SCHOOL?
DON'T YOU KNOW THAT FLETCHLING CAN'T PARTICIPATE IN SKY BATTLES? HAVEN'T YOU STUDIED UP ON IT?
I GUESS NOT.
YOU COME TO CLASS UNPREPARED WITHOUT YOUR BOOKS, AFTER ALL.
GLARE
FWAP
I FOUND THIS IN THE HALL...
...SO I KEPT IT FOR YOU.
HERE.
Y TRAINER DATA BOOK
TH...
THANK... YOU.
HUH?
DROP

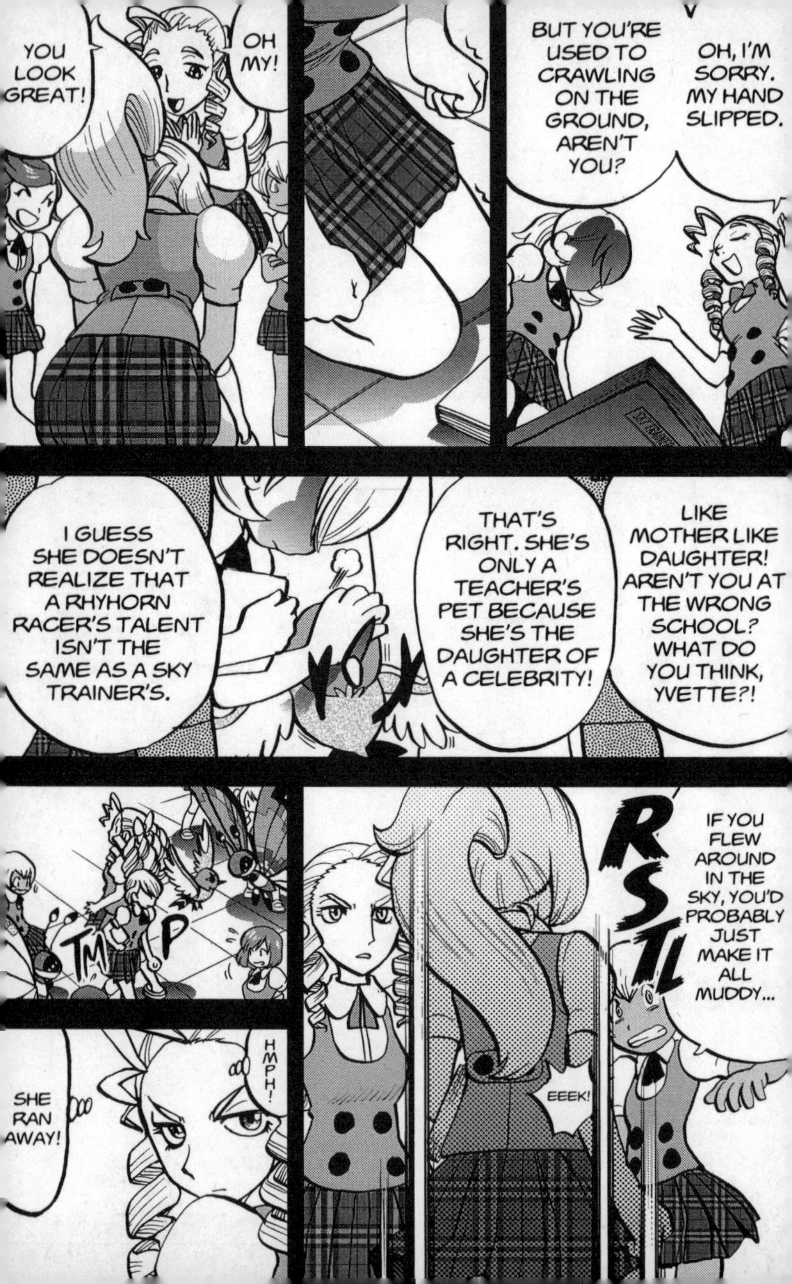
OH, I'M SORRY. MY HAND SLIPPED.
BUT YOU'RE USED TO CRAWLING ON THE GROUND, AREN'T YOU?
OH MY!
YOU LOOK GREAT!
LIKE MOTHER LIKE DAUGHTER! AREN'T YOU AT THE WRONG SCHOOL? WHAT DO YOU THINK, YVETTE?!
THAT'S RIGHT. SHE'S ONLY A TEACHER'S PET BECAUSE SHE'S THE DAUGHTER OF A CELEBRITY!
I GUESS SHE DOESN'T REALIZE THAT A RHYHORN RACER'S TALENT ISN'T THE SAME AS A SKY TRAINER'S.
IF YOU FLEW AROUND IN THE SKY, YOU'D PROBABLY JUST MAKE IT ALL MUDDY...
RSTL
EEEK!
TMP
HMPH!
SHE RAN AWAY!

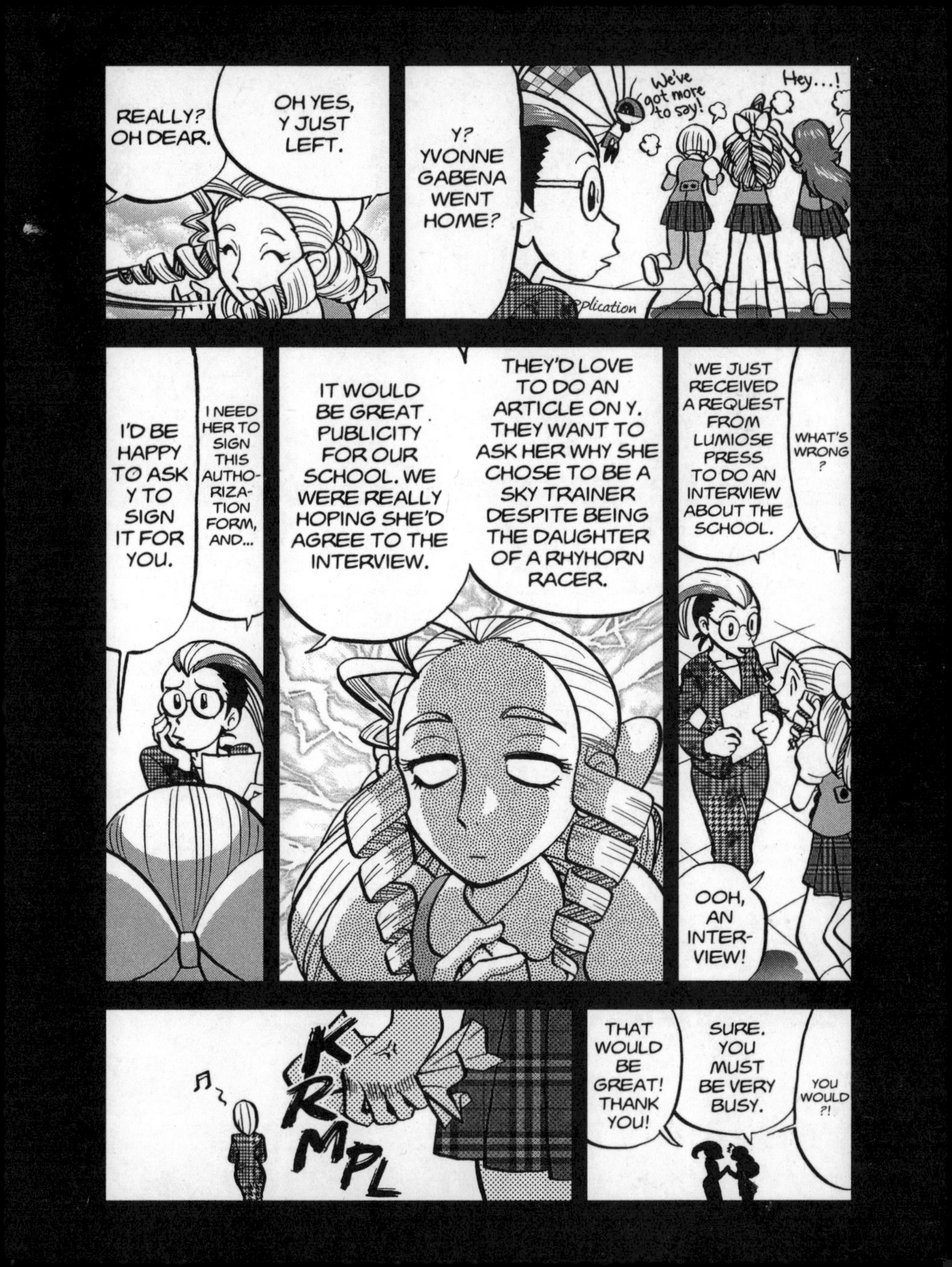
Hey...!
We've got more to say!
Y? YVONNE GABENA WENT HOME?
OH YES, Y JUST LEFT.
REALLY? OH DEAR.
WHAT'S WRONG?
WE JUST RECEIVED A REQUEST FROM LUMIOSE PRESS TO DO AN INTERVIEW ABOUT THE SCHOOL.
OOH, AN INTER-VIEW!
THEY'D LOVE TO DO AN ARTICLE ON Y. THEY WANT TO ASK HER WHY SHE CHOSE TO BE A SKY TRAINER DESPITE BEING THE DAUGHTER OF A RHYHORN RACER.
IT WOULD BE GREAT PUBLICITY FOR OUR SCHOOL. WE WERE REALLY HOPING SHE'D AGREE TO THE INTERVIEW.
I NEED HER TO SIGN THIS AUTHO-RIZA-TION FORM, AND...
I'D BE HAPPY TO ASK Y TO SIGN IT FOR YOU.
YOU WOULD?!
SURE. YOU MUST BE VERY BUSY.
THAT WOULD BE GREAT! THANK YOU!
KRMPL

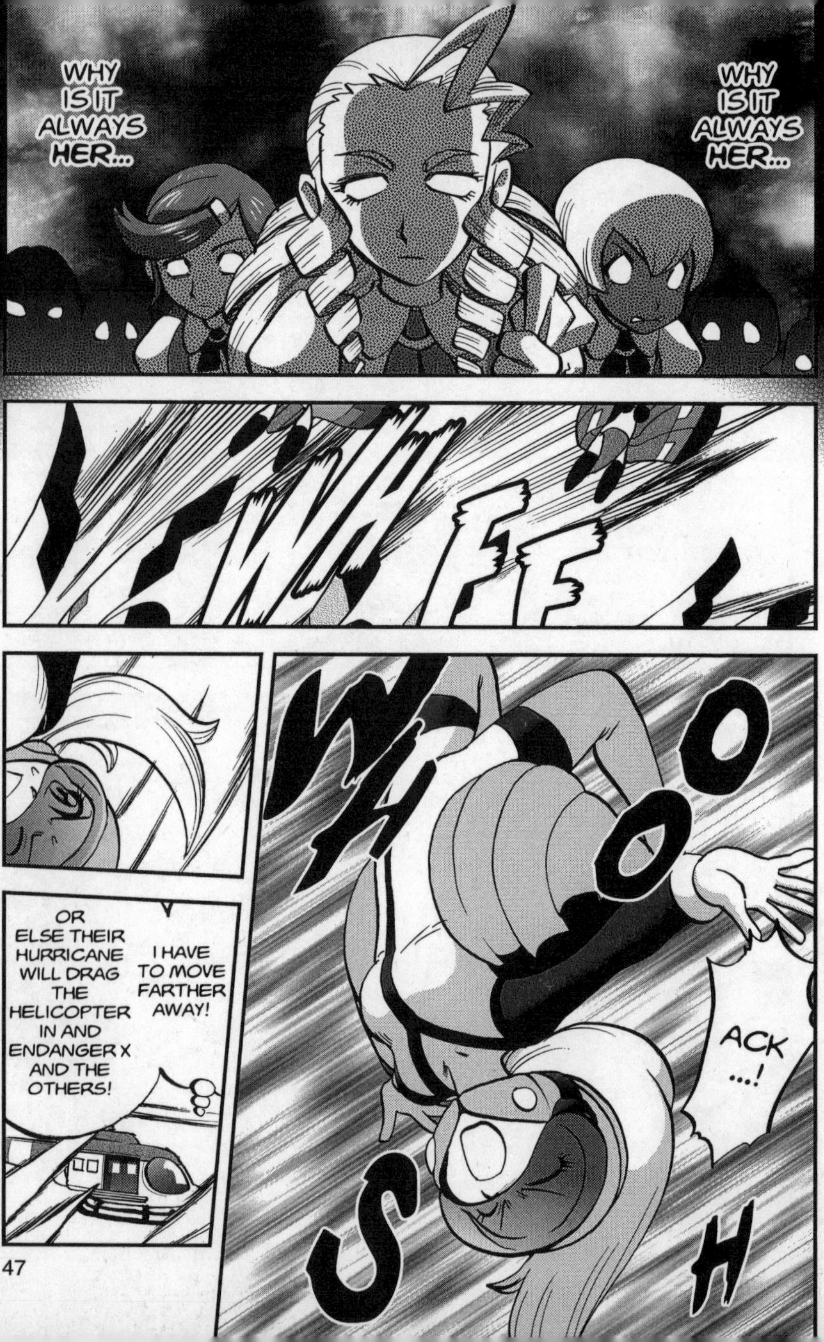
WHY IS IT ALWAYS HER...
WHY IS IT ALWAYS HER...
WHFF
WHOOOSH
ACK ...!
I HAVE TO MOVE FARTHER AWAY!
OR ELSE THEIR HURRICANE WILL DRAG THE HELICOPTER IN AND ENDANGER X AND THE OTHERS!

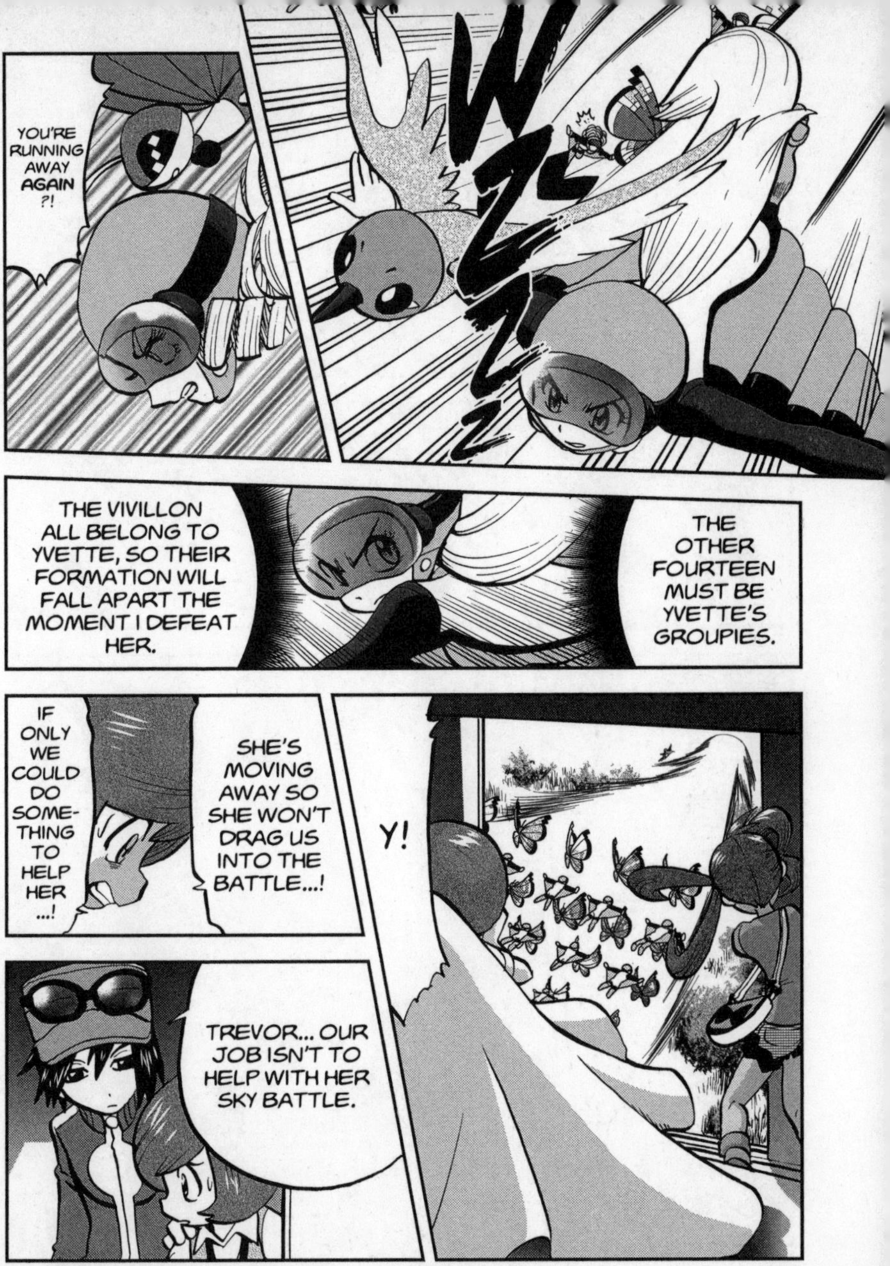
YOU'RE RUNNING AWAY AGAIN?!
THE OTHER FOURTEEN MUST BE YVETTE'S GROUPIES.
THE VIVILLON ALL BELONG TO YVETTE, SO THEIR FORMATION WILL FALL APART THE MOMENT I DEFEAT HER.
Y!
SHE'S MOVING AWAY SO SHE WON'T DRAG US INTO THE BATTLE...!
IF ONLY WE COULD DO SOME-THING TO HELP HER...!
TREVOR... OUR JOB ISN'T TO HELP WITH HER SKY BATTLE.

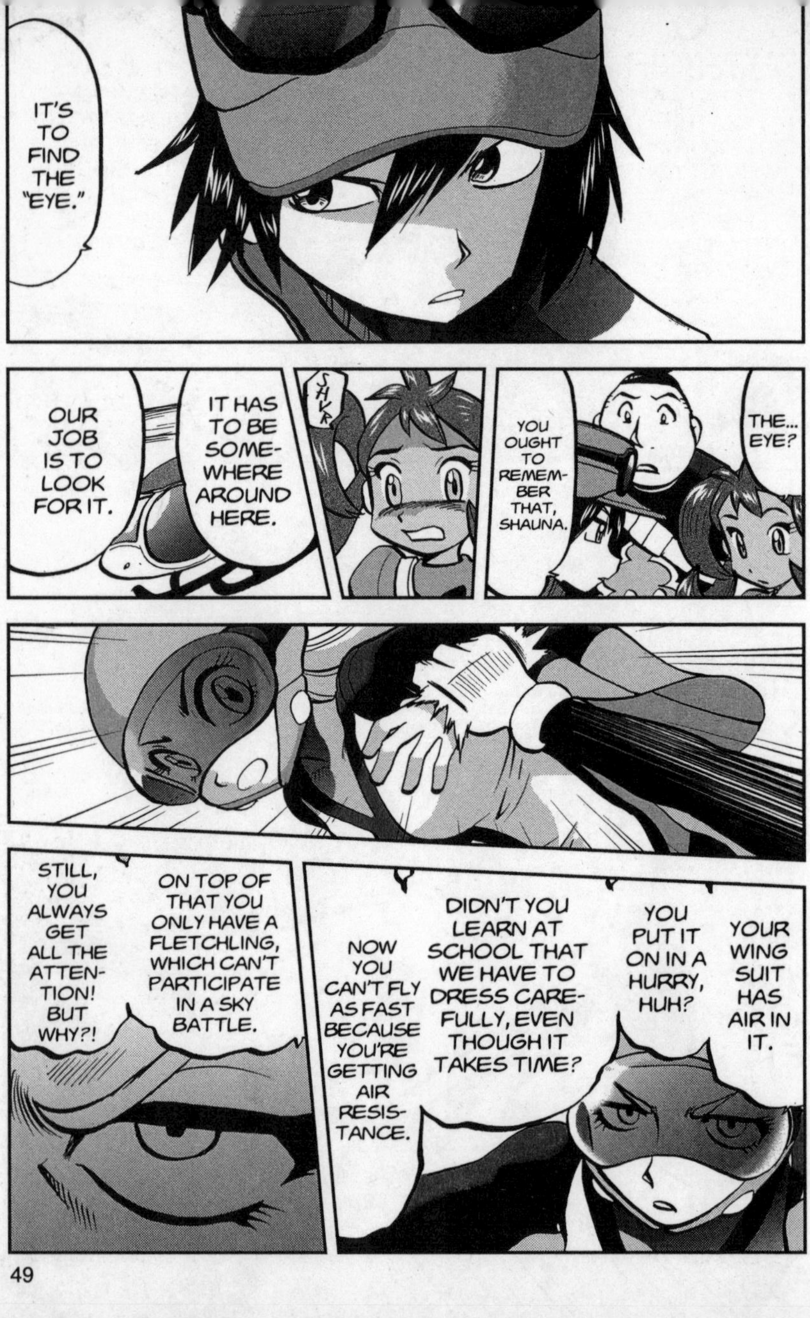

IT'S TO FIND THE "EYE."
THE... EYE?
YOU OUGHT TO REMEMBER THAT, SHAUNA.
SHVR
IT HAS TO BE SOMEWHERE AROUND HERE.
OUR JOB IS TO LOOK FOR IT.
YOUR WING SUIT HAS AIR IN IT.
YOU PUT IT ON IN A HURRY, HUH?
DIDN'T YOU LEARN AT SCHOOL THAT WE HAVE TO DRESS CAREFULLY, EVEN THOUGH IT TAKES TIME?
NOW YOU CAN'T FLY AS FAST BECAUSE YOU'RE GETTING AIR RESISTANCE.
ON TOP OF THAT YOU ONLY HAVE A FLETCHLING, WHICH CAN'T PARTICIPATE IN A SKY BATTLE.
STILL, YOU ALWAYS GET ALL THE ATTENTION! BUT WHY?!

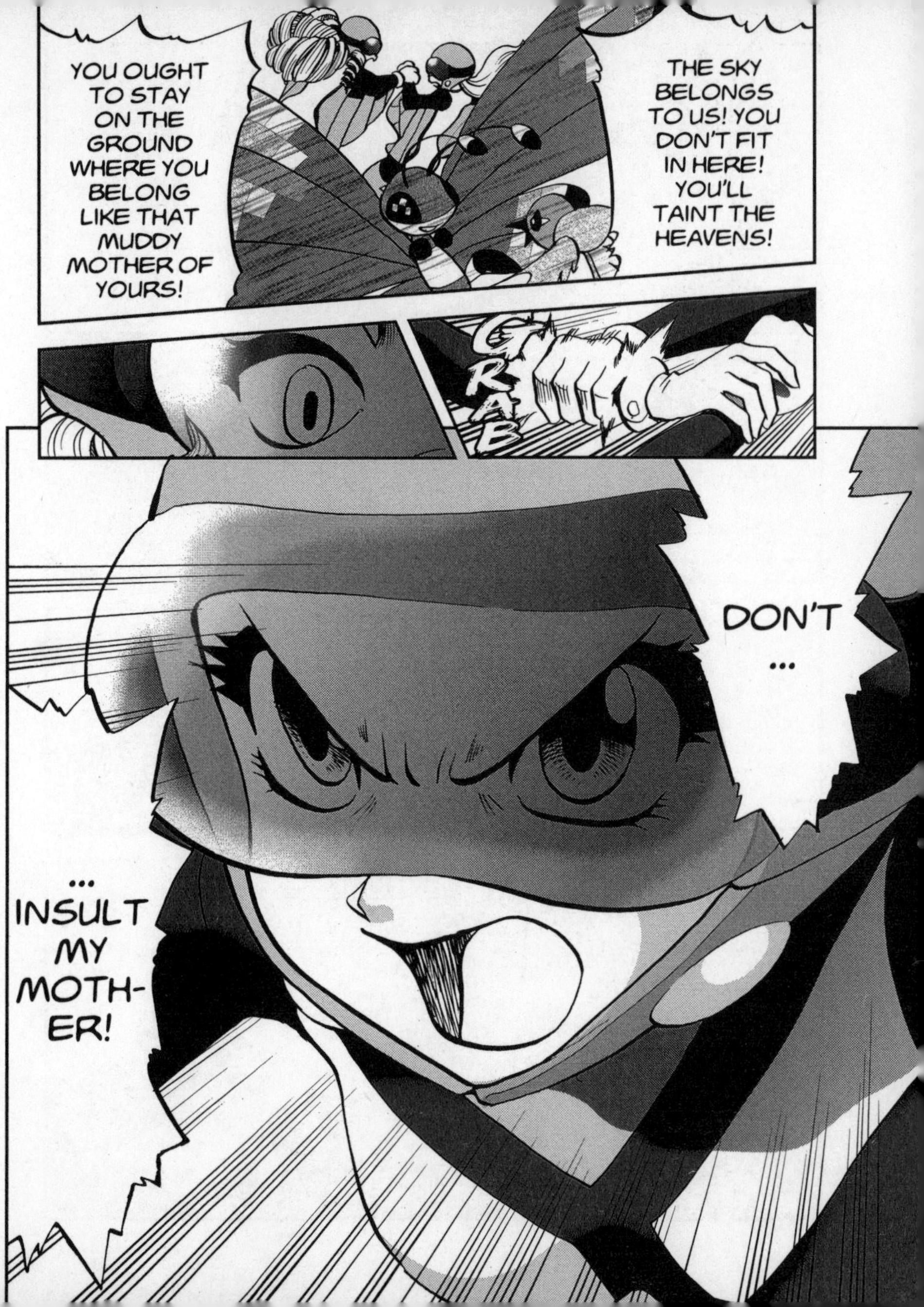
THE SKY BELONGS TO US! YOU DON'T FIT IN HERE! YOU'LL TAINT THE HEAVENS!
YOU OUGHT TO STAY ON THE GROUND WHERE YOU BELONG LIKE THAT MUDDY MOTHER OF YOURS!
GRAB
DON'T ...
... INSULT MY MOTH-ER!

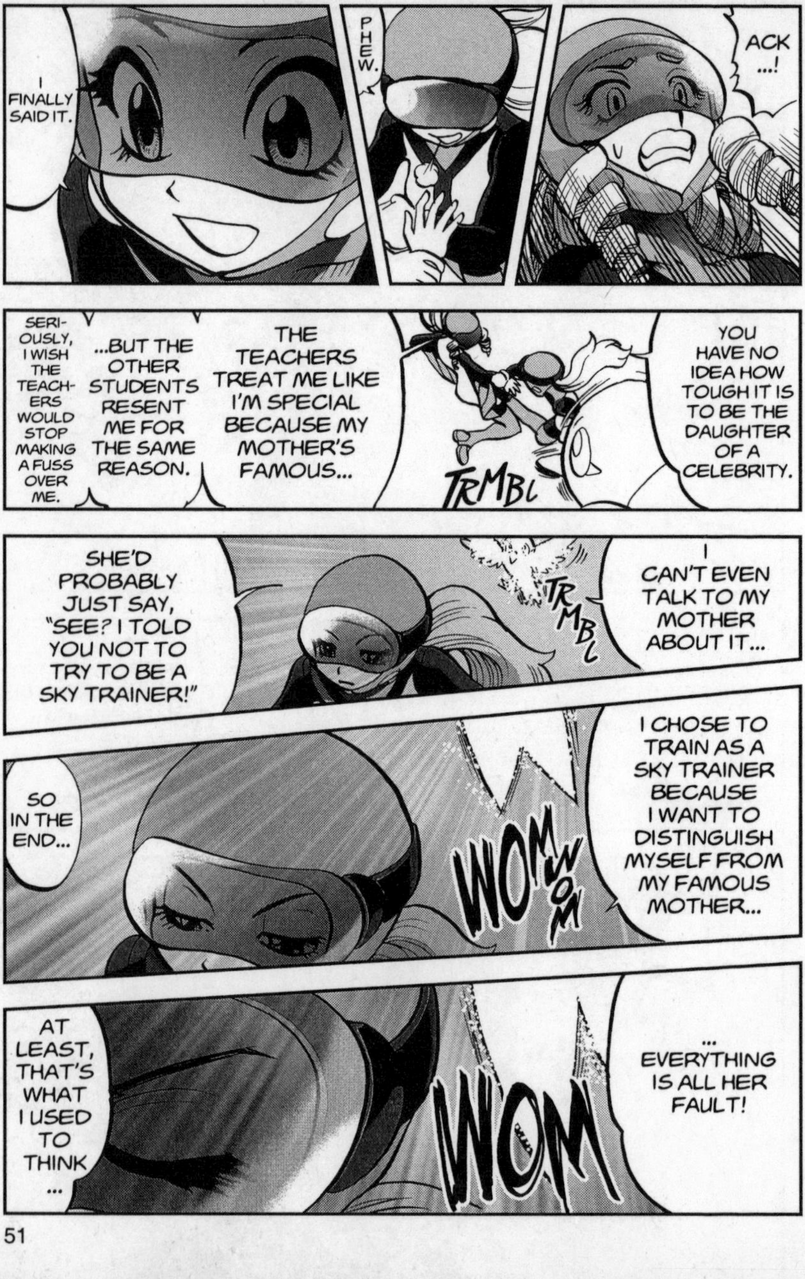

ACK ...!
PHEW.
I FINALLY SAID IT.
YOU HAVE NO IDEA HOW TOUGH IT IS TO BE THE DAUGHTER OF A CELEBRITY.
TRMBL
THE TEACHERS TREAT ME LIKE I'M SPECIAL BECAUSE MY MOTHER'S FAMOUS...
...BUT THE OTHER STUDENTS RESENT ME FOR THE SAME REASON.
SERI-OUSLY, I WISH THE TEACH-ERS WOULD STOP MAKING A FUSS OVER ME.
I CAN'T EVEN TALK TO MY MOTHER ABOUT IT...
TRMBL
SHE'D PROBABLY JUST SAY, "SEE? I TOLD YOU NOT TO TRY TO BE A SKY TRAINER!"
I CHOSE TO TRAIN AS A SKY TRAINER BECAUSE I WANT TO DISTINGUISH MYSELF FROM MY FAMOUS MOTHER...
WOM WOM WOM
SO IN THE END...
...EVERYTHING IS ALL HER FAULT!
WOM
AT LEAST, THAT'S WHAT I USED TO THINK ...

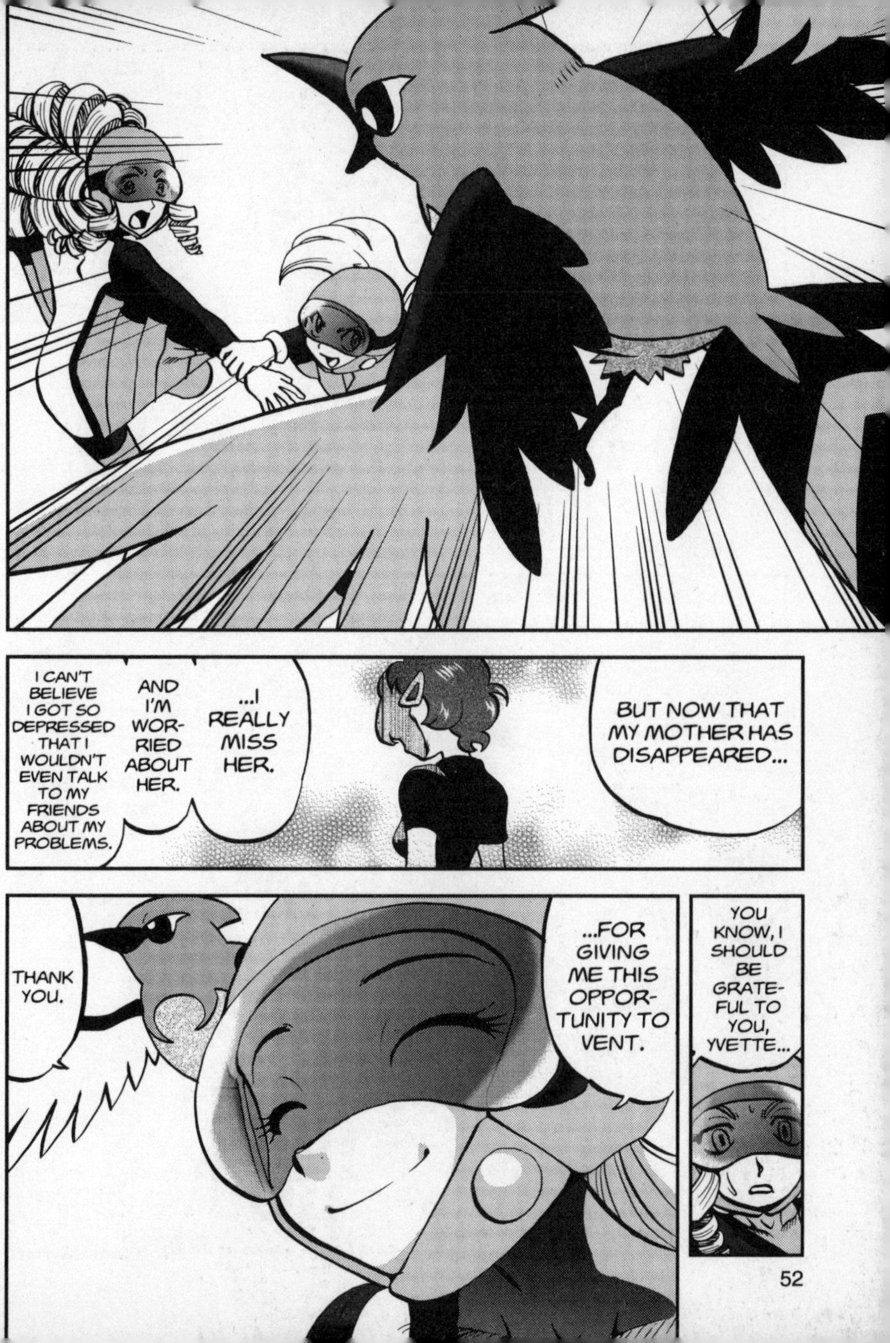
BUT NOW THAT MY MOTHER HAS DISAPPEARED...
...I REALLY MISS HER.
AND I'M WORRIED ABOUT HER.
I CAN'T BELIEVE I GOT SO DEPRESSED THAT I WOULDN'T EVEN TALK TO MY FRIENDS ABOUT MY PROBLEMS.
YOU KNOW, I SHOULD BE GRATEFUL TO YOU, YVETTE...
...FOR GIVING ME THIS OPPORTUNITY TO VENT.
THANK YOU.

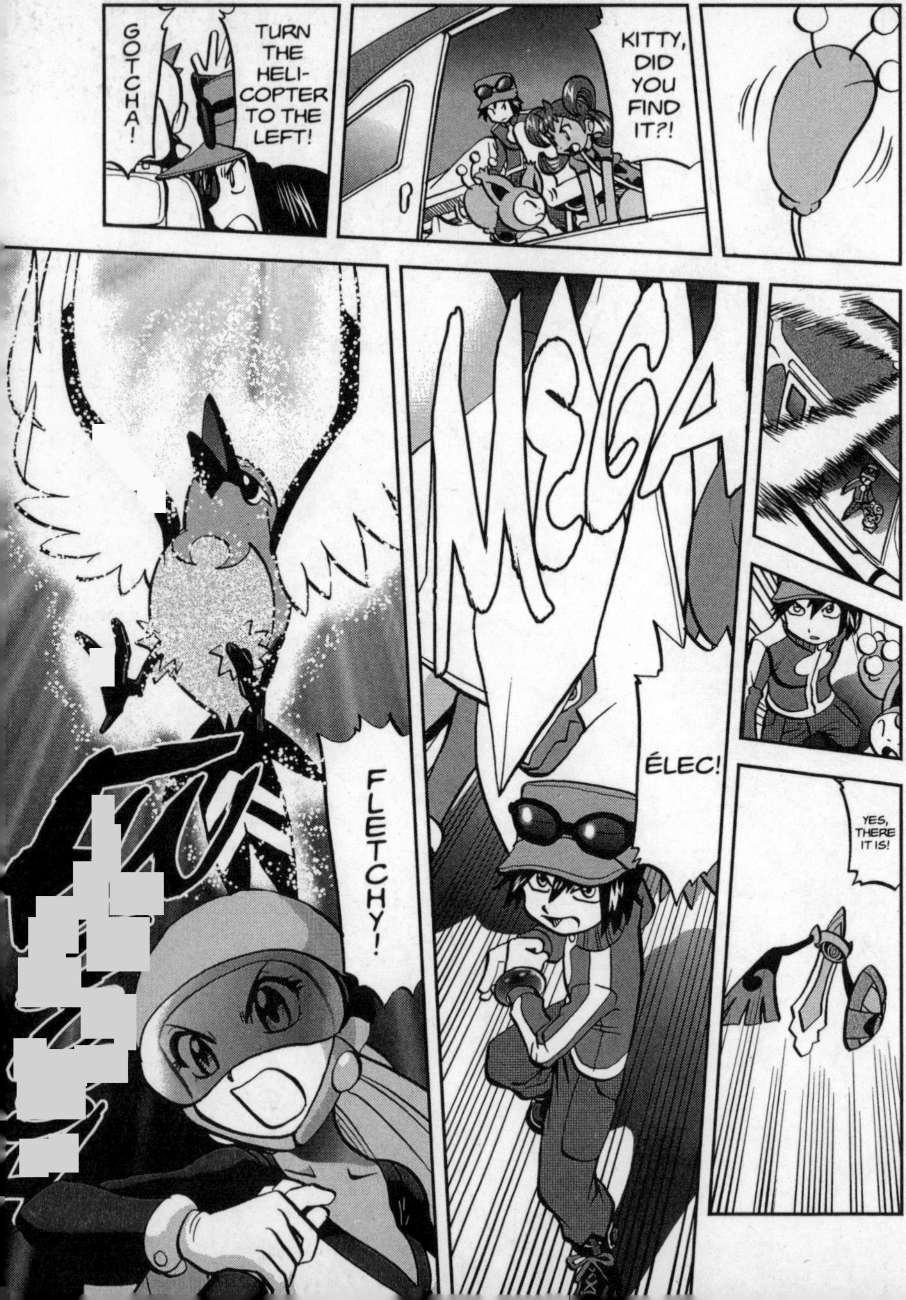
KITTY, DID YOU FIND IT?!
TURN THE HELI-COPTER TO THE LEFT!
GOTCHA!
YES, THERE IT IS!
MEGA
ÉLEC!
FLETCHY!

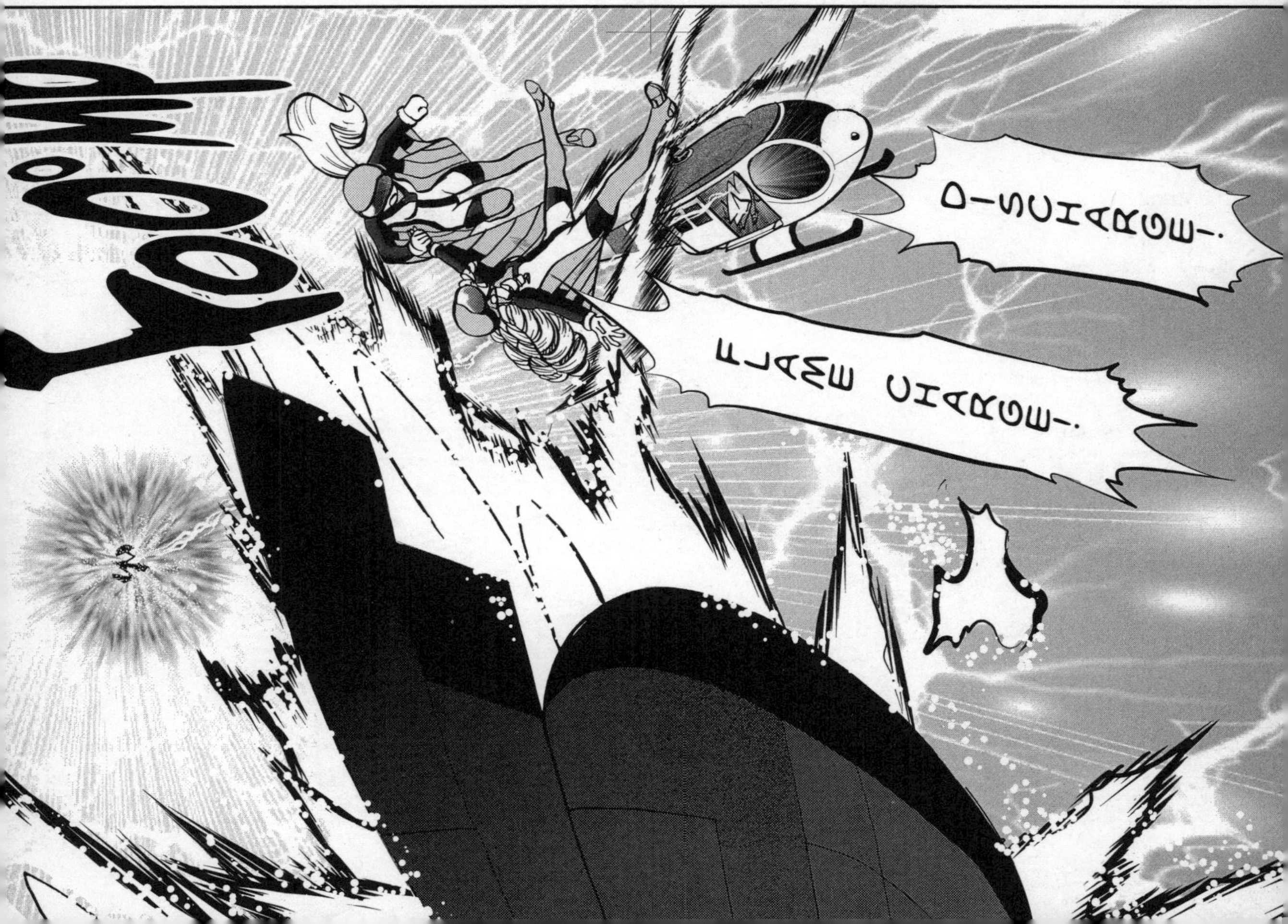
DISCHARGE!
FLAME CHARGE!
FOOOMP

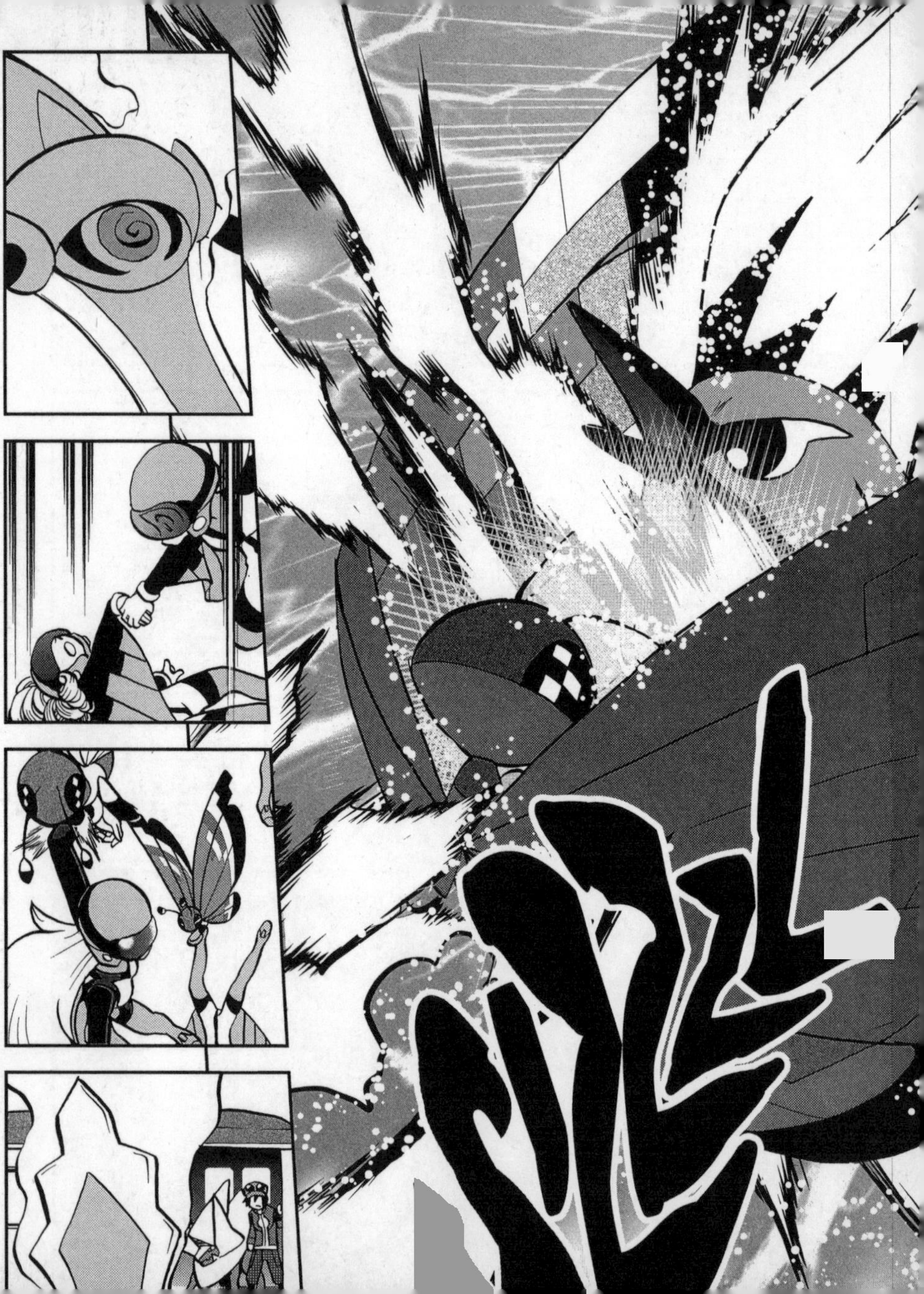

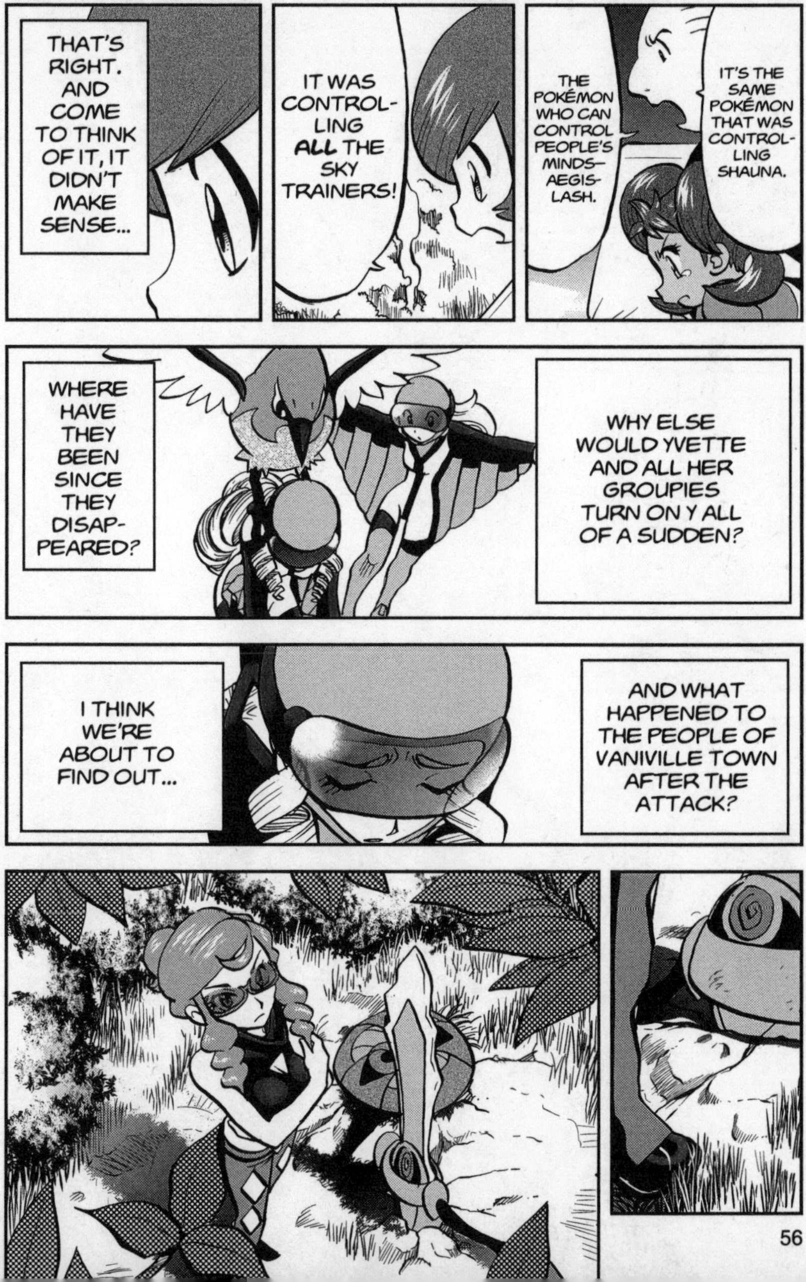
IT'S THE SAME POKÉMON THAT WAS CONTROL-LING SHAUNA.
THE POKÉMON WHO CAN CONTROL PEOPLE'S MINDS—AEGIS-LASH.
IT WAS CONTROL-LING **ALL** THE SKY TRAINERS!
THAT'S RIGHT. AND COME TO THINK OF IT, IT DIDN'T MAKE SENSE...
WHY ELSE WOULD YVETTE AND ALL HER GROUPIES TURN ON Y ALL OF A SUDDEN?
WHERE HAVE THEY BEEN SINCE THEY DISAP-PEARED?
AND WHAT HAPPENED TO THE PEOPLE OF VANIVILLE TOWN AFTER THE ATTACK?
I THINK WE'RE ABOUT TO FIND OUT...

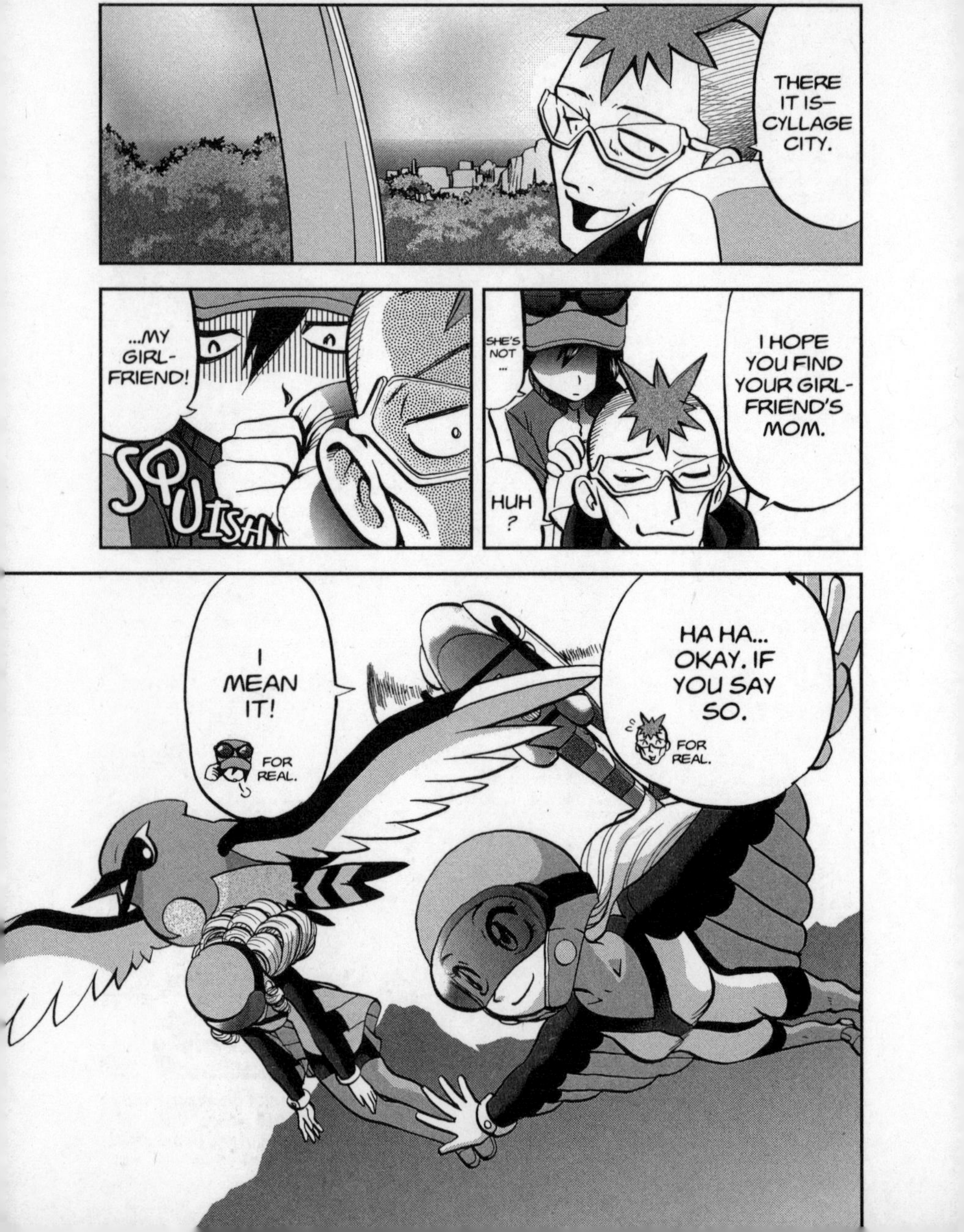
THERE IT IS— CYLLAGE CITY.
I HOPE YOU FIND YOUR GIRL-FRIEND'S MOM.
SHE'S NOT ...
HUH ?
...MY GIRL-FRIEND!
SQUISH
HA HA... OKAY. IF YOU SAY SO.
FOR REAL.
I MEAN IT!
FOR REAL.

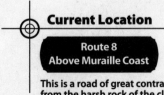

Current Location

Route 8
Above Muraille Coast

This is a road of great contrasts,
from the harsh rock of the cliffs to
the soft sands of the beach.
* They're taking the air route.

Adventure 17 Shooting Frogadier

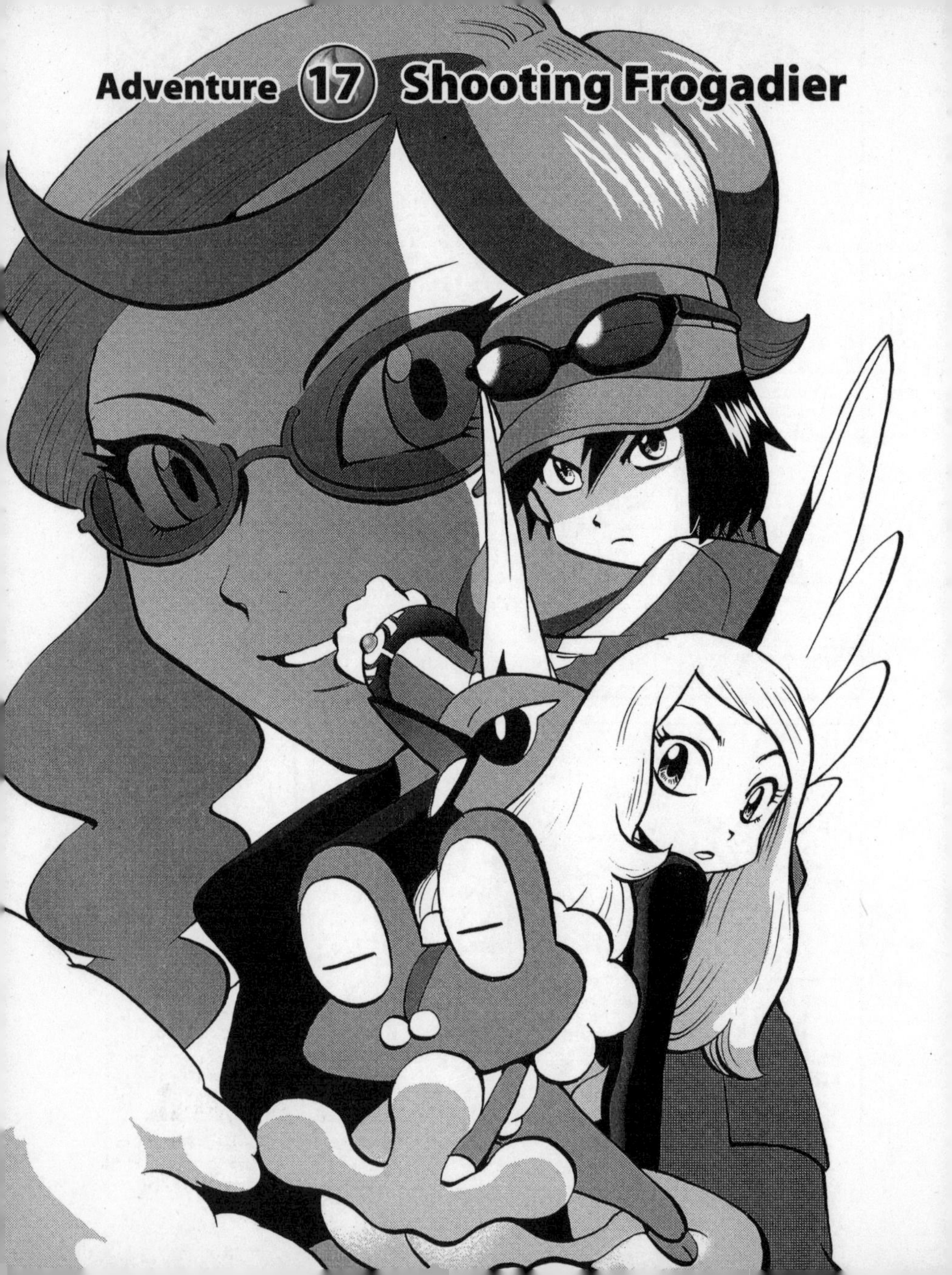

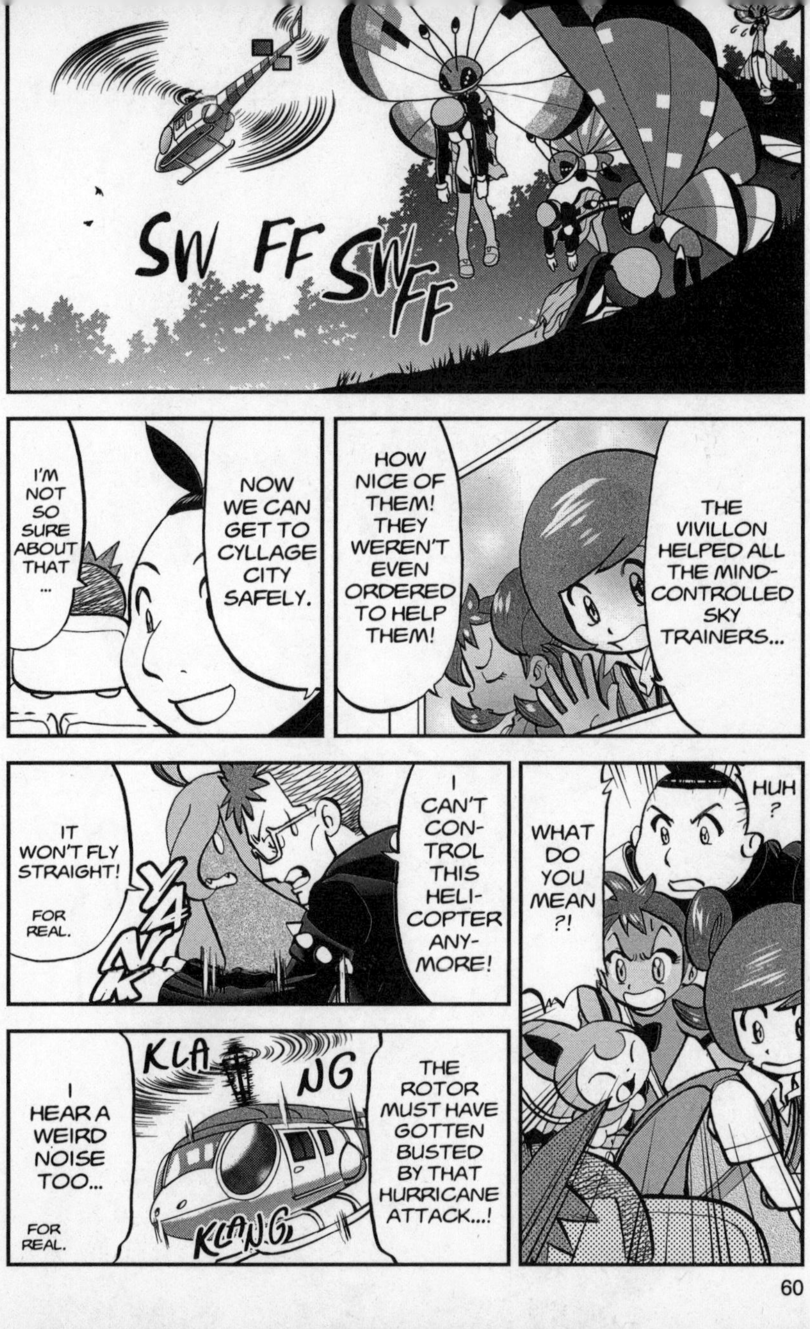
SWFF
SWFF
THE VIVILLON HELPED ALL THE MIND-CONTROLLED SKY TRAINERS...
HOW NICE OF THEM! THEY WEREN'T EVEN ORDERED TO HELP THEM!
NOW WE CAN GET TO CYLLAGE CITY SAFELY.
I'M NOT SO SURE ABOUT THAT...
HUH?
WHAT DO YOU MEAN?!
I CAN'T CONTROL THIS HELICOPTER ANYMORE!
YANK
IT WON'T FLY STRAIGHT!
FOR REAL.
THE ROTOR MUST HAVE GOTTEN BUSTED BY THAT HURRICANE ATTACK...!
KLANG
I HEAR A WEIRD NOISE TOO...
FOR REAL.
KLANG

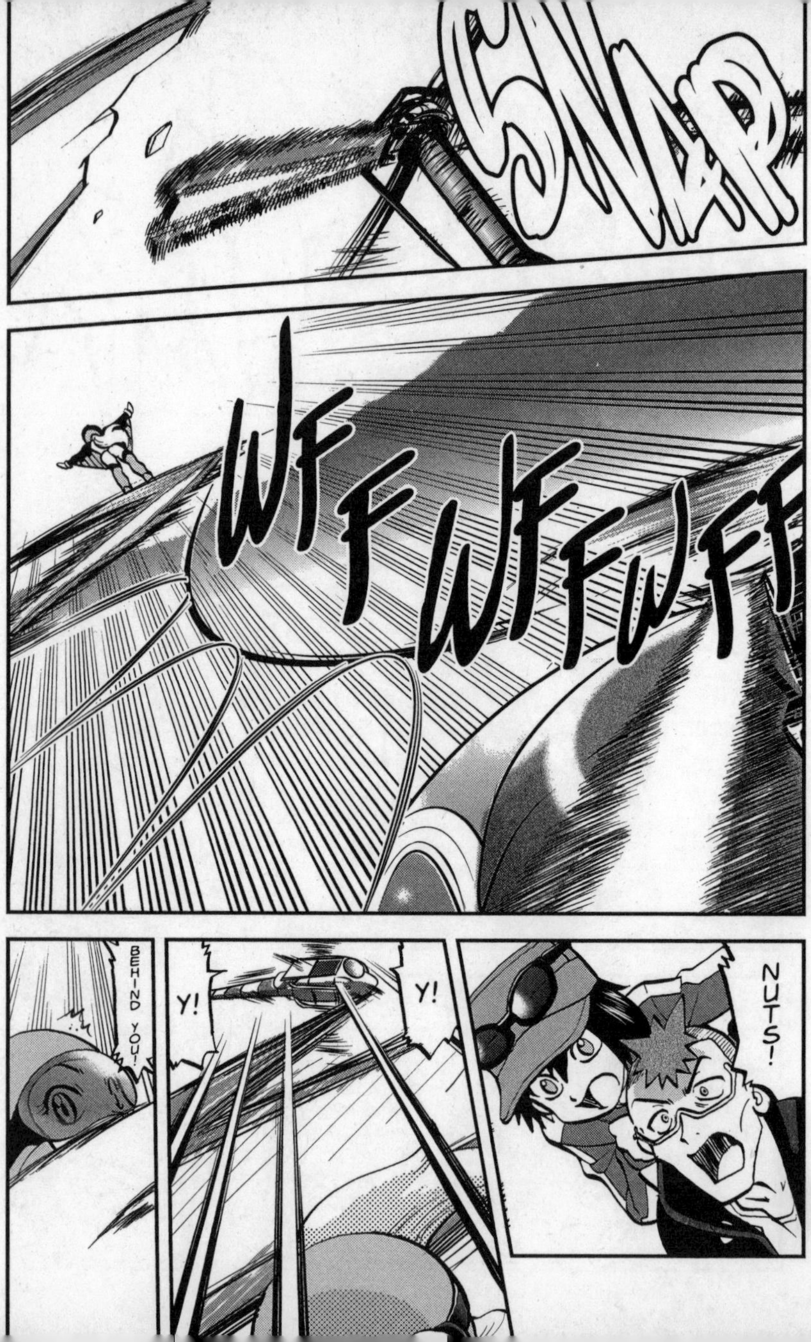
SNAP
WFF WFF WFF
NUTS!
Y!
Y!
BEHIND YOU!

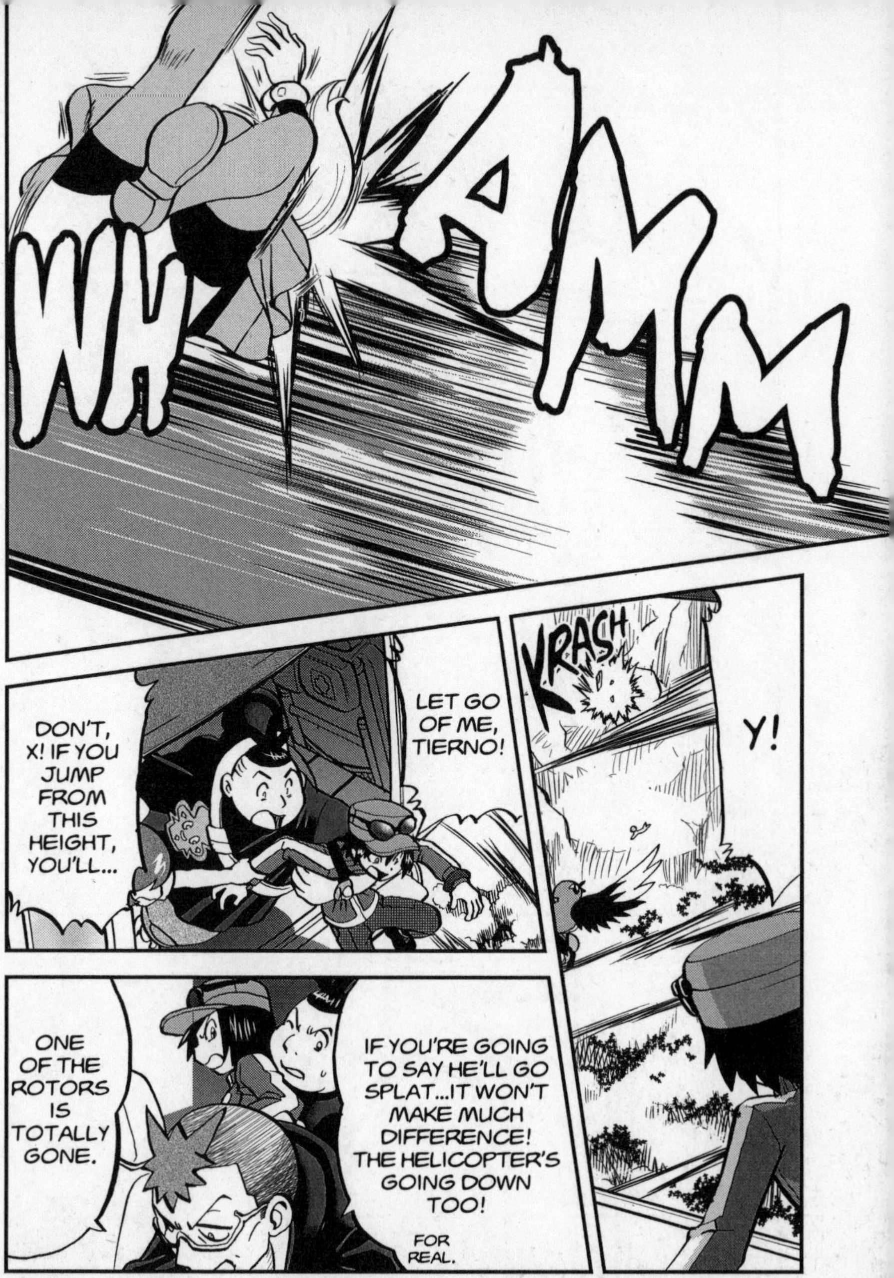

WHAMM
KRASH
Y!
LET GO OF ME, TIERNO!
DON'T, X! IF YOU JUMP FROM THIS HEIGHT, YOU'LL...
IF YOU'RE GOING TO SAY HE'LL GO SPLAT...IT WON'T MAKE MUCH DIFFERENCE! THE HELICOPTER'S GOING DOWN TOO!
FOR REAL.
ONE OF THE ROTORS IS TOTALLY GONE.

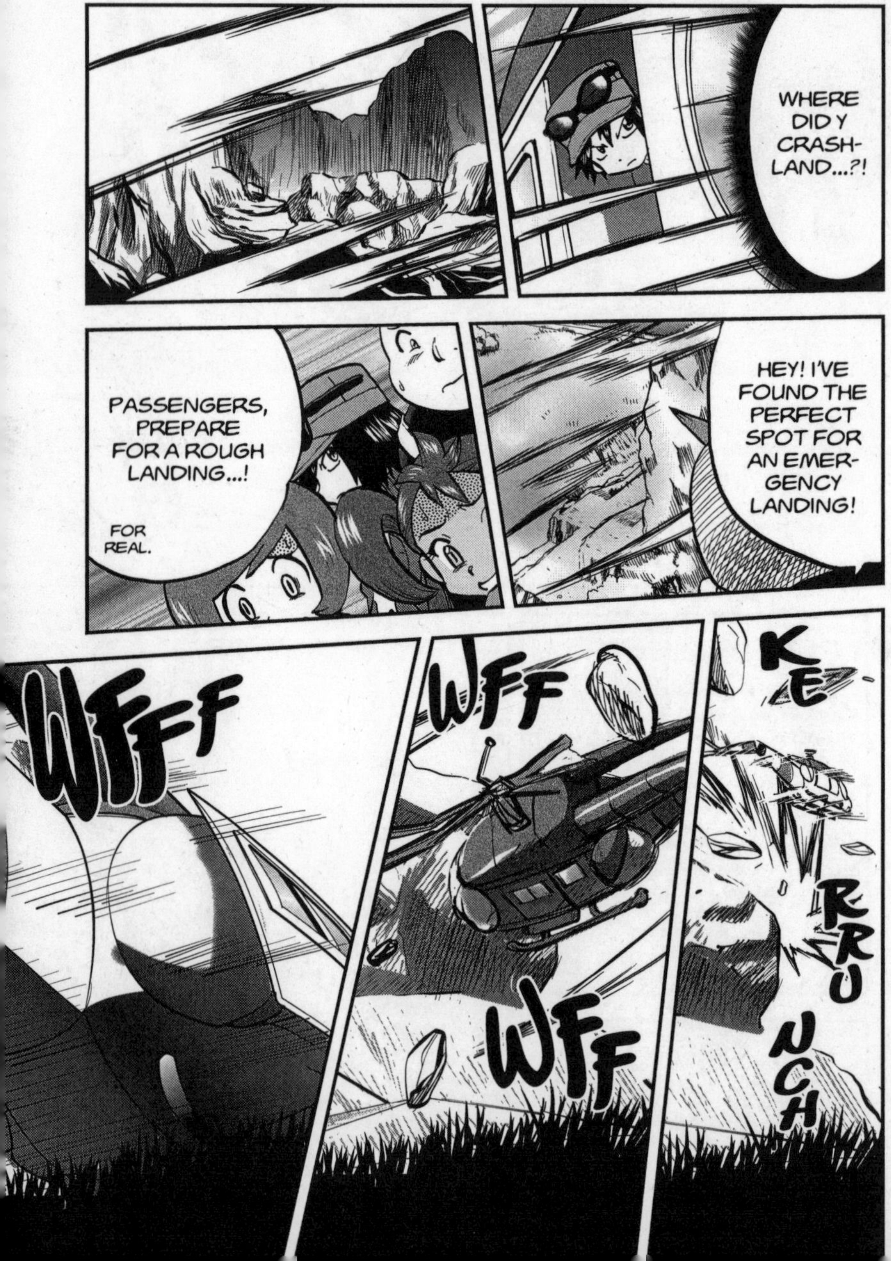
WHERE DID Y CRASH-LAND...?!
HEY! I'VE FOUND THE PERFECT SPOT FOR AN EMERGENCY LANDING!
PASSENGERS, PREPARE FOR A ROUGH LANDING...!
FOR REAL.
KE
RRRU
NCH
WFF
WFF
WFFF

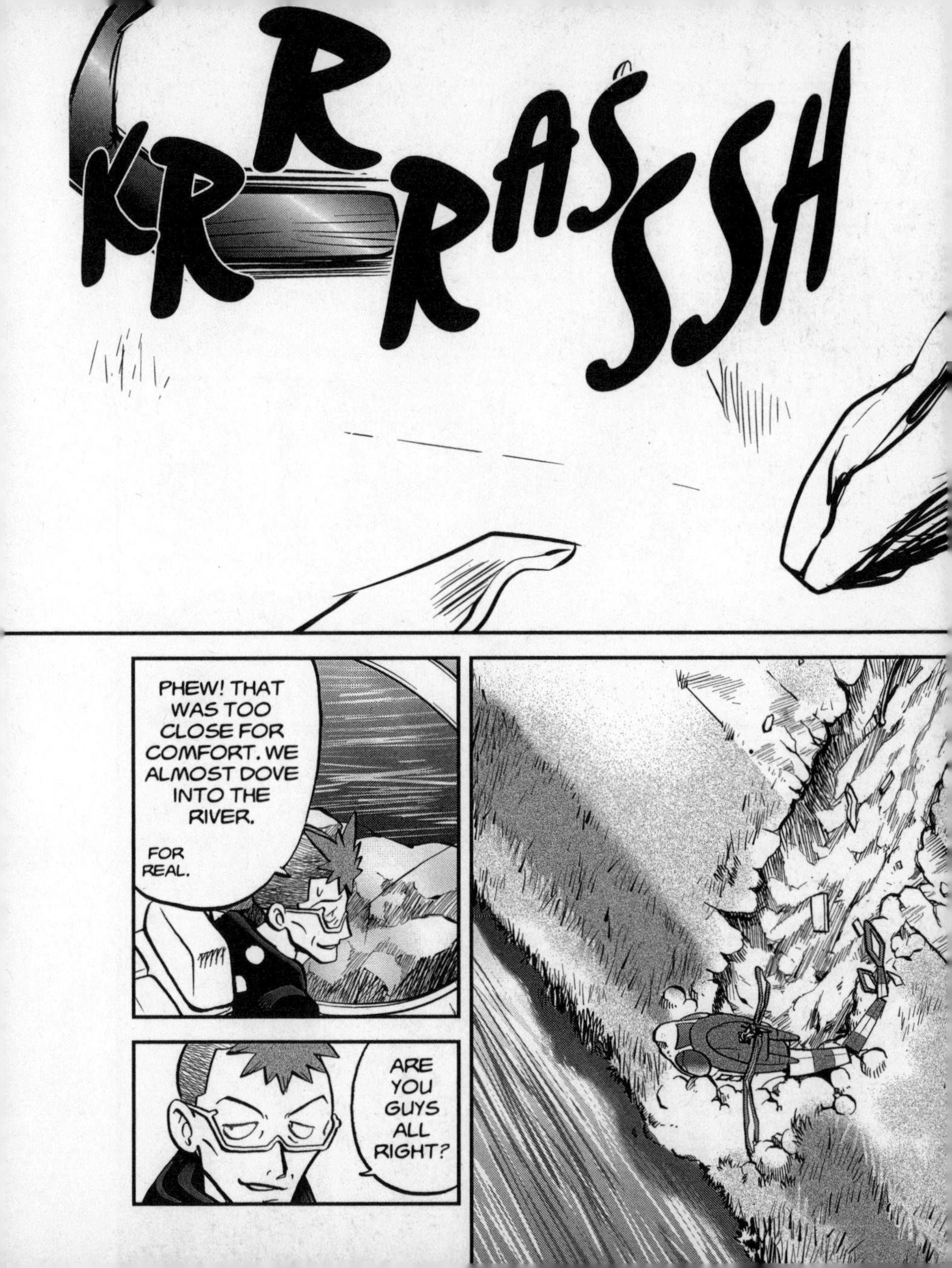
KRRRASSSH
PHEW! THAT WAS TOO CLOSE FOR COMFORT. WE ALMOST DOVE INTO THE RIVER.
FOR REAL.
ARE YOU GUYS ALL RIGHT?

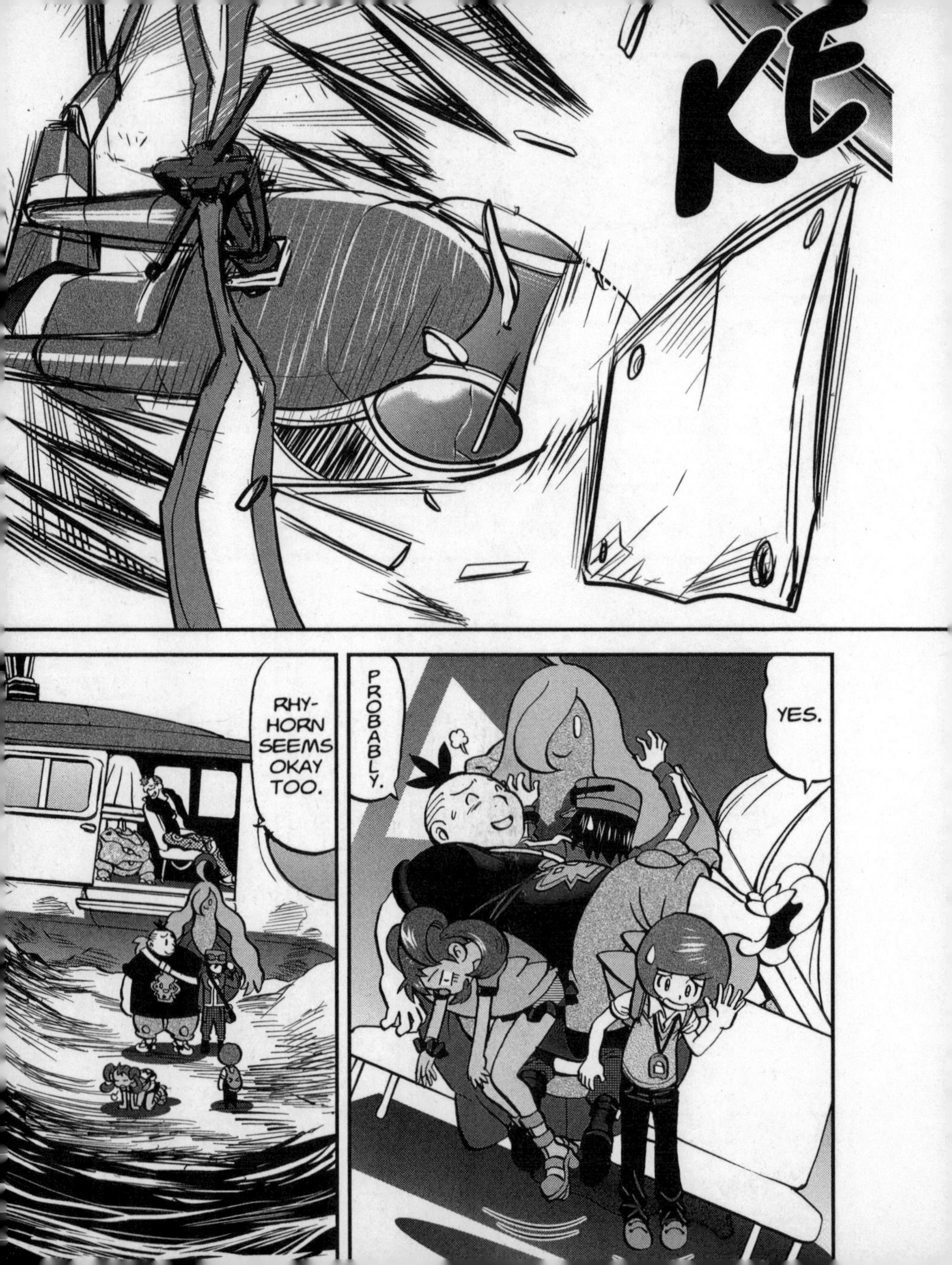
KE
YES.
PROBABLY.
RHY-HORN SEEMS OKAY TOO.

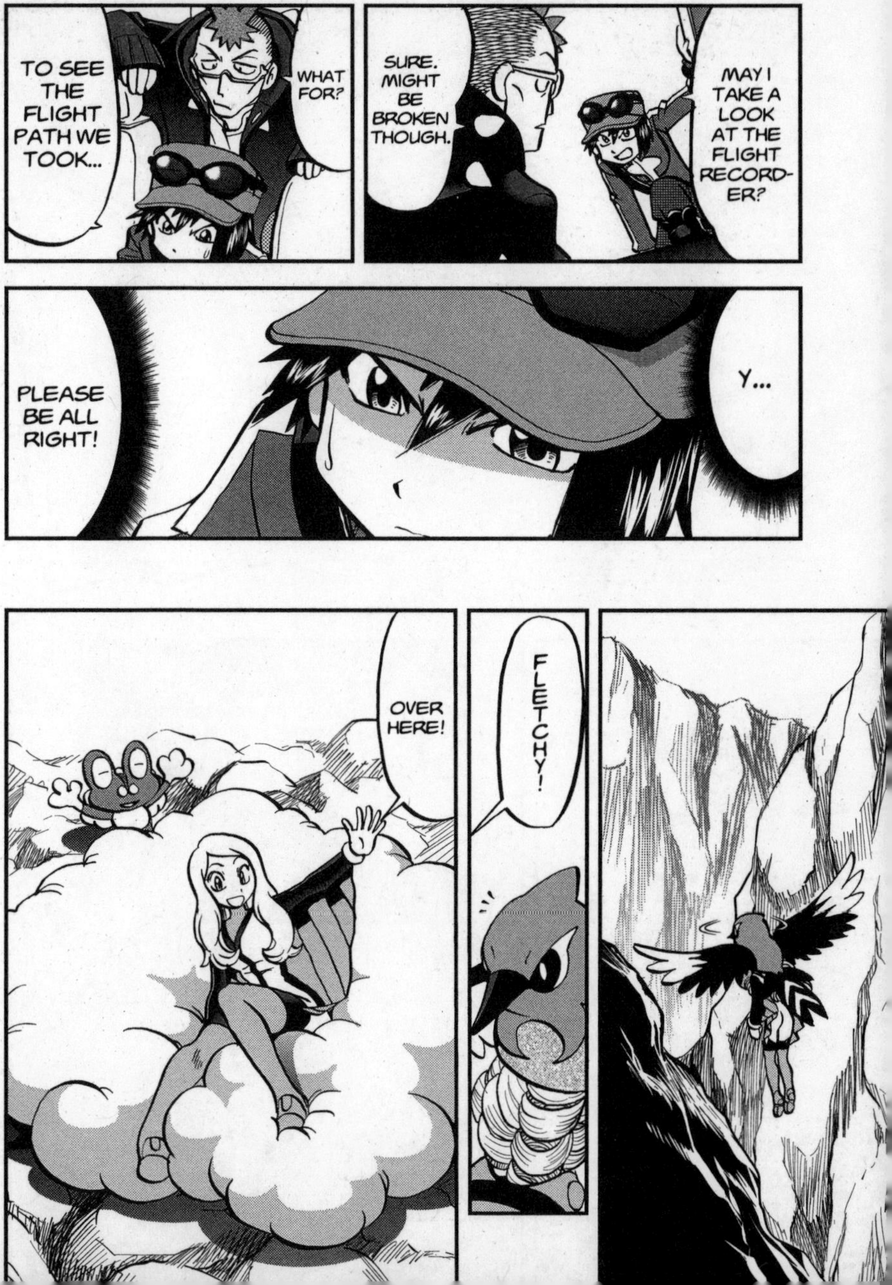
MAY I TAKE A LOOK AT THE FLIGHT RECORDER?
SURE. MIGHT BE BROKEN THOUGH.
WHAT FOR?
TO SEE THE FLIGHT PATH WE TOOK...
Y...
PLEASE BE ALL RIGHT!
FLETCHY!
OVER HERE!

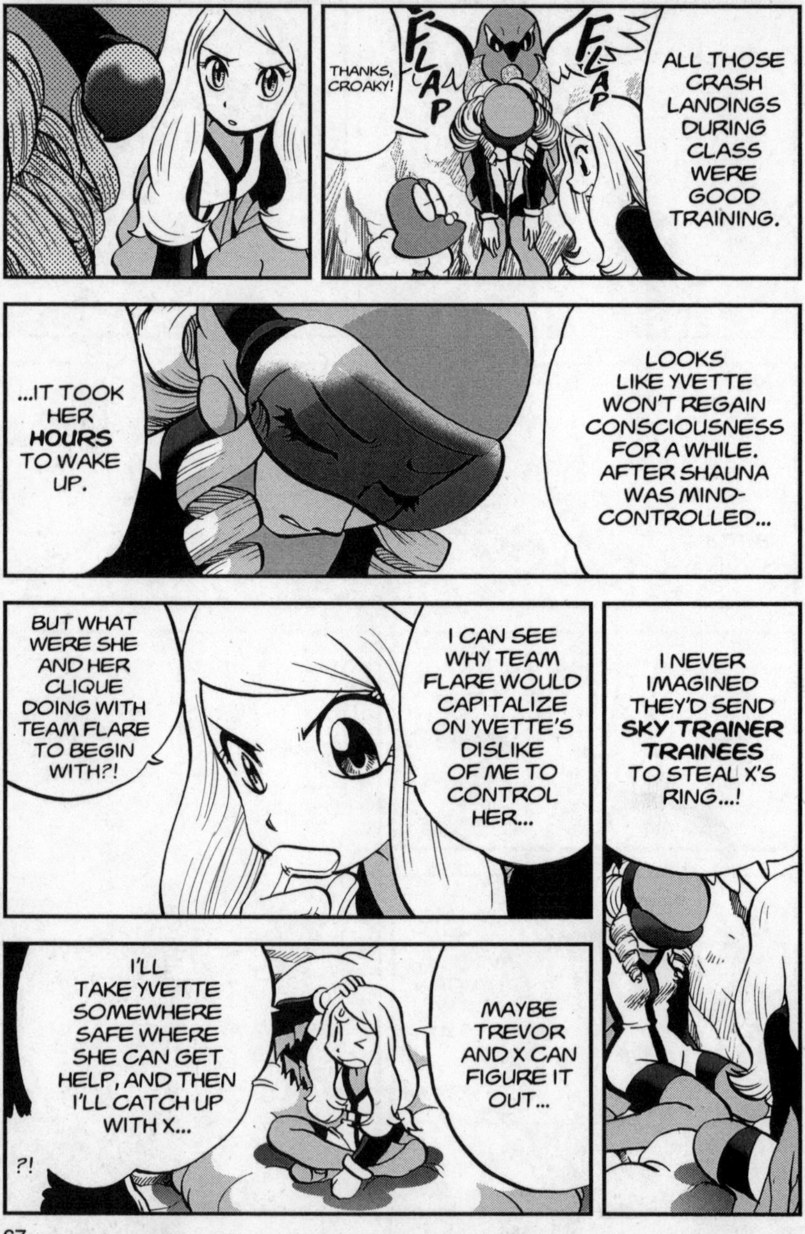
FLAP
FLAP
ALL THOSE CRASH LANDINGS DURING CLASS WERE GOOD TRAINING.
THANKS, CROAKY!
LOOKS LIKE YVETTE WON'T REGAIN CONSCIOUSNESS FOR A WHILE. AFTER SHAUNA WAS MIND-CONTROLLED...
...IT TOOK HER **HOURS** TO WAKE UP.
I NEVER IMAGINED THEY'D SEND **SKY TRAINER TRAINEES** TO STEAL X'S RING...!
I CAN SEE WHY TEAM FLARE WOULD CAPITALIZE ON YVETTE'S DISLIKE OF ME TO CONTROL HER...
BUT WHAT WERE SHE AND HER CLIQUE DOING WITH TEAM FLARE TO BEGIN WITH?!
MAYBE TREVOR AND X CAN FIGURE IT OUT...
I'LL TAKE YVETTE SOMEWHERE SAFE WHERE SHE CAN GET HELP, AND THEN I'LL CATCH UP WITH X...
?!

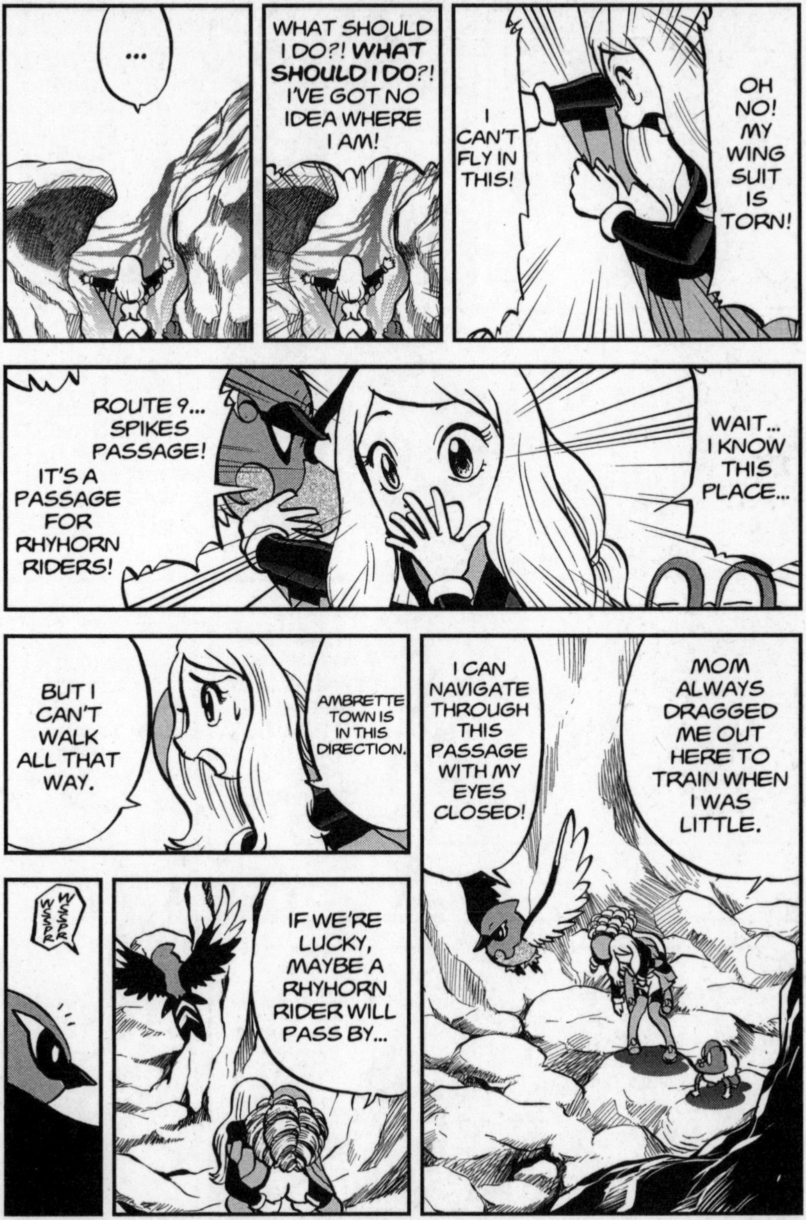
OH NO! MY WING SUIT IS TORN!
I CAN'T FLY IN THIS!
WHAT SHOULD I DO?! WHAT SHOULD I DO?! I'VE GOT NO IDEA WHERE I AM!
...
WAIT... I KNOW THIS PLACE...
ROUTE 9... SPIKES PASSAGE!
IT'S A PASSAGE FOR RHYHORN RIDERS!
MOM ALWAYS DRAGGED ME OUT HERE TO TRAIN WHEN I WAS LITTLE.
I CAN NAVIGATE THROUGH THIS PASSAGE WITH MY EYES CLOSED!
AMBRETTE TOWN IS IN THIS DIRECTION.
BUT I CAN'T WALK ALL THAT WAY.
IF WE'RE LUCKY, MAYBE A RHYHORN RIDER WILL PASS BY...
WSSPR WSSPR

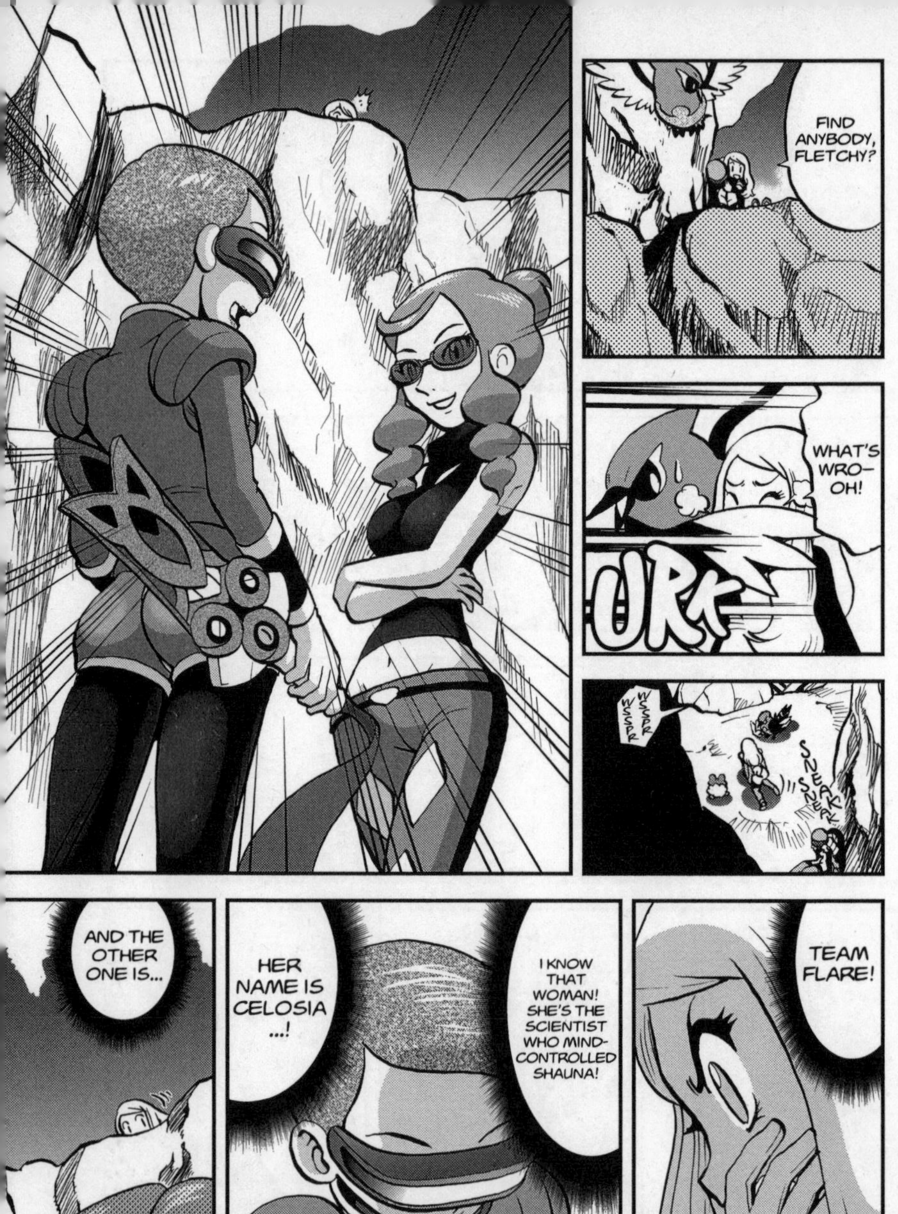
FIND ANYBODY, FLETCHY?
WHAT'S WRO— OH!
URK
WSSPR WSSPR
SNEAK SNEAK
TEAM FLARE!
I KNOW THAT WOMAN! SHE'S THE SCIENTIST WHO MIND-CONTROLLED SHAUNA!
HER NAME IS CELOSIA ...!
AND THE OTHER ONE IS...

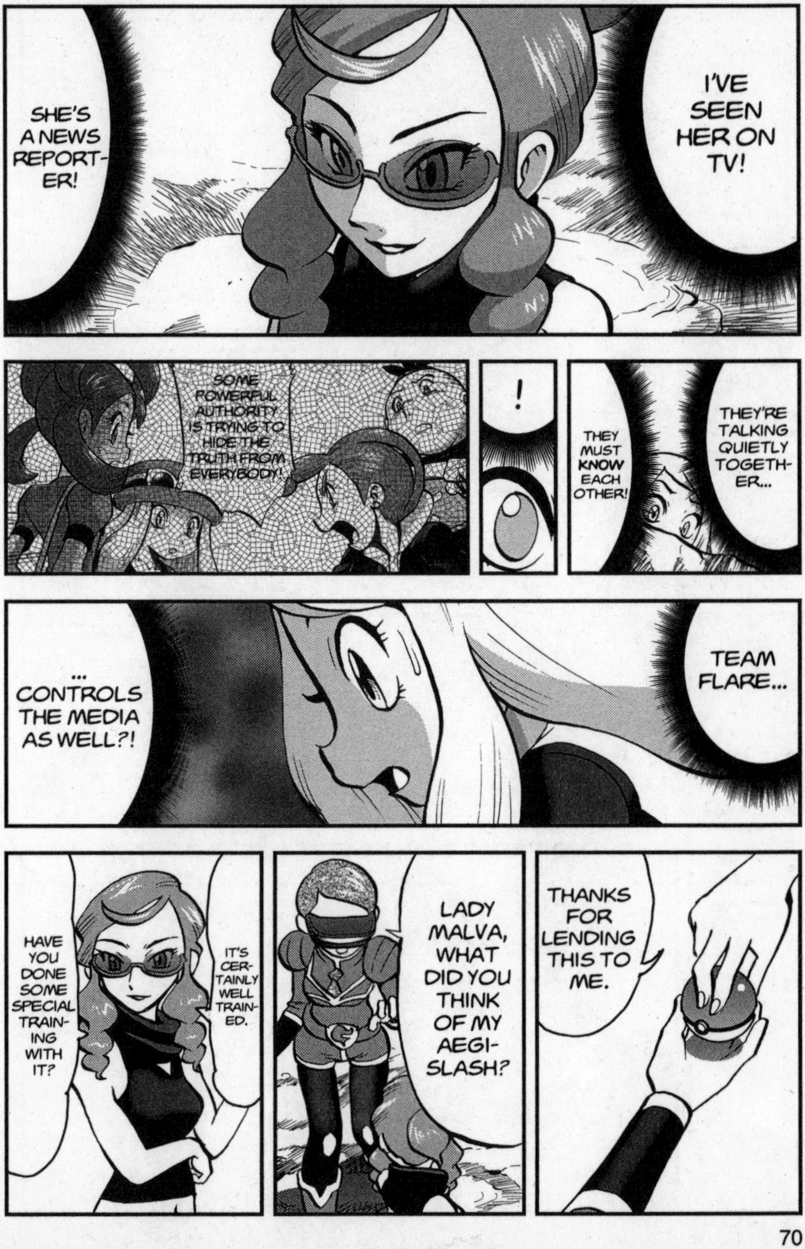
I'VE SEEN HER ON TV!
SHE'S A NEWS REPORTER!
THEY'RE TALKING QUIETLY TOGETHER...
THEY MUST **KNOW** EACH OTHER!
!
SOME POWERFUL AUTHORITY IS TRYING TO HIDE THE TRUTH FROM EVERYBODY!
TEAM FLARE...
...CONTROLS THE MEDIA AS WELL?!
THANKS FOR LENDING THIS TO ME.
LADY MALVA, WHAT DID YOU THINK OF MY AEGISLASH?
IT'S CERTAINLY WELL TRAINED.
HAVE YOU DONE SOME SPECIAL TRAINING WITH IT?

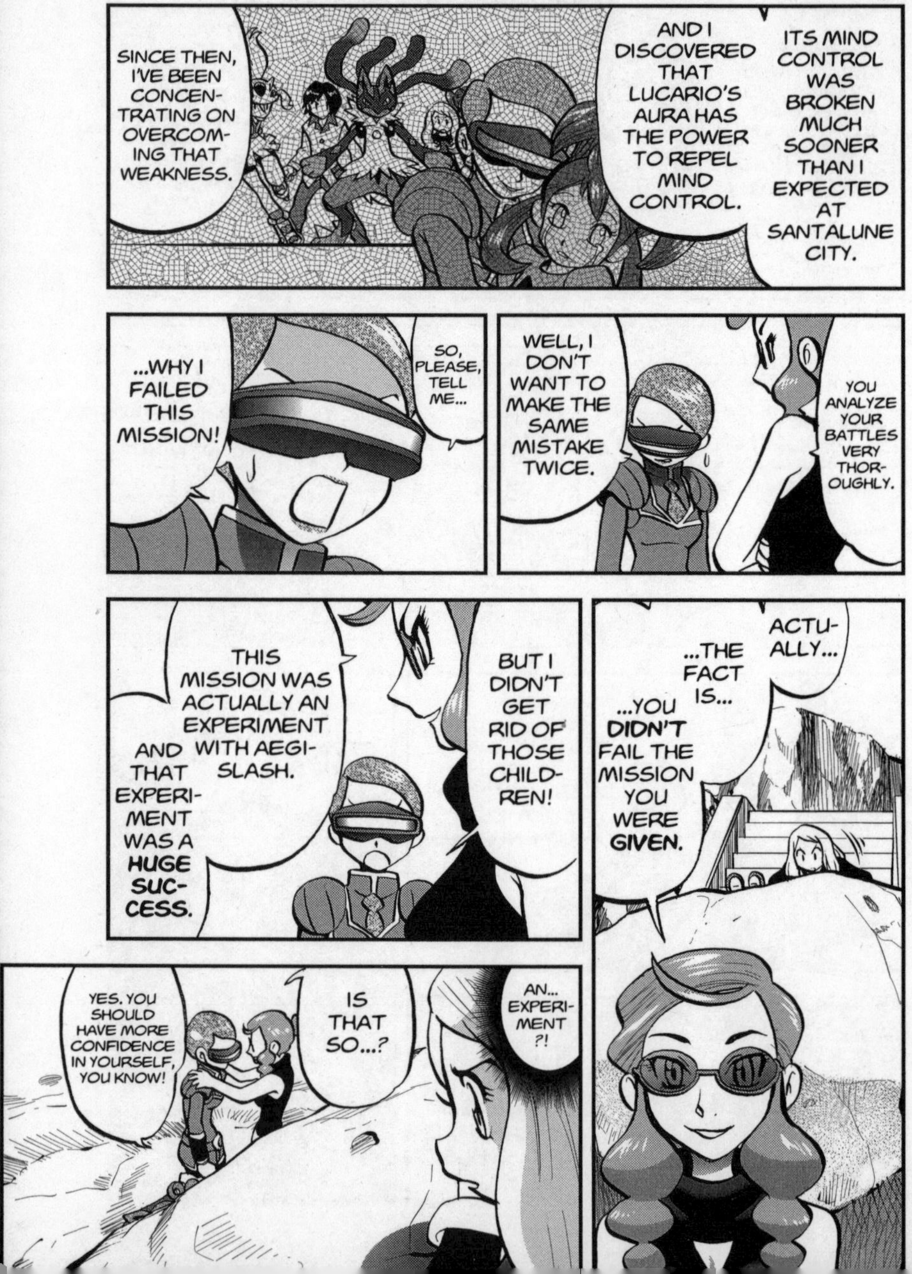
ITS MIND CONTROL WAS BROKEN MUCH SOONER THAN I EXPECTED AT SANTALUNE CITY.
AND I DISCOVERED THAT LUCARIO'S AURA HAS THE POWER TO REPEL MIND CONTROL.
SINCE THEN, I'VE BEEN CONCENTRATING ON OVERCOMING THAT WEAKNESS.
YOU ANALYZE YOUR BATTLES VERY THOROUGHLY.
WELL, I DON'T WANT TO MAKE THE SAME MISTAKE TWICE.
SO, PLEASE, TELL ME...
...WHY I FAILED THIS MISSION!
ACTUALLY...
...THE FACT IS...
...YOU **DIDN'T** FAIL THE MISSION YOU WERE **GIVEN.**
BUT I DIDN'T GET RID OF THOSE CHILDREN!
THIS MISSION WAS ACTUALLY AN EXPERIMENT WITH AEGISLASH.
AND THAT EXPERIMENT WAS A **HUGE SUCCESS.**
AN... EXPERIMENT?!
IS THAT SO...?
YES. YOU SHOULD HAVE MORE CONFIDENCE IN YOURSELF, YOU KNOW!

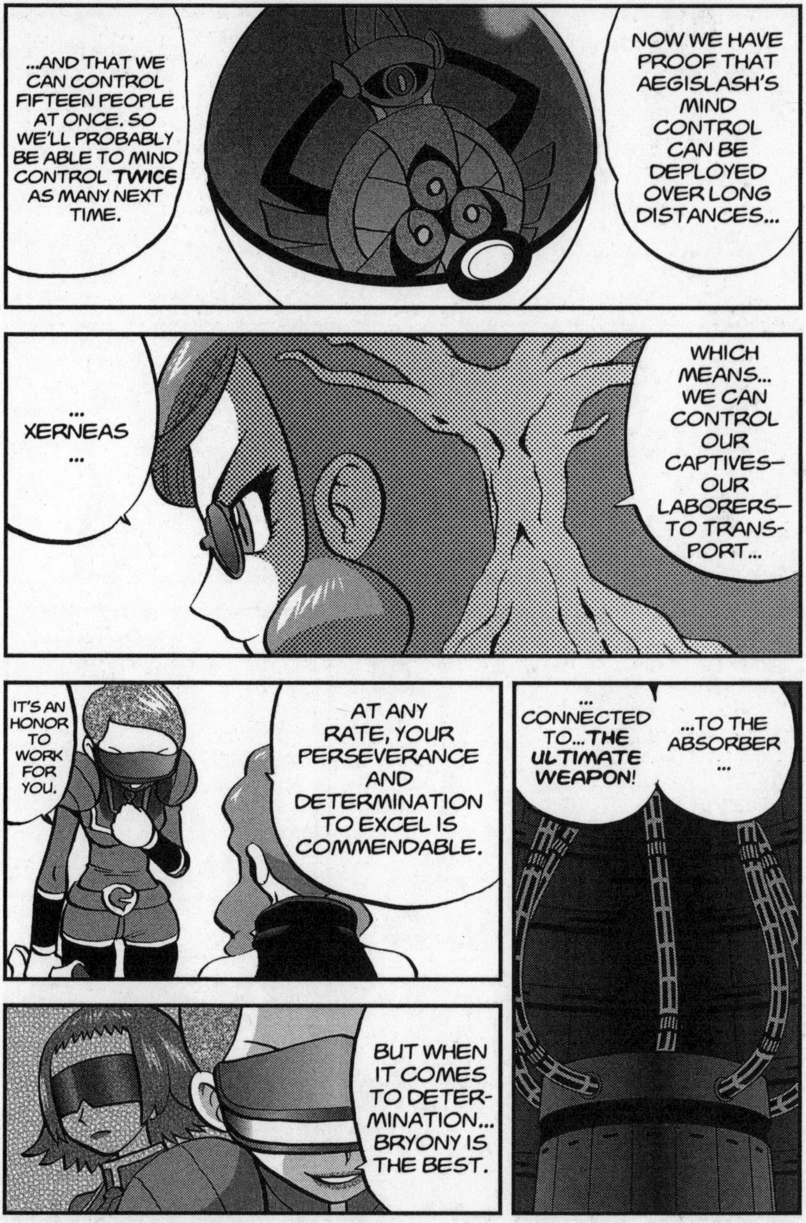
NOW WE HAVE PROOF THAT AEGISLASH'S MIND CONTROL CAN BE DEPLOYED OVER LONG DISTANCES...
...AND THAT WE CAN CONTROL FIFTEEN PEOPLE AT ONCE. SO WE'LL PROBABLY BE ABLE TO MIND CONTROL **TWICE** AS MANY NEXT TIME.
WHICH MEANS... WE CAN CONTROL OUR CAPTIVES—OUR LABORERS—TO TRANS-PORT...
... XERNEAS ...
...TO THE ABSORBER ...
... CONNECTED TO... **THE ULTIMATE WEAPON!**
AT ANY RATE, YOUR PERSEVERANCE AND DETERMINATION TO EXCEL IS COMMENDABLE.
IT'S AN HONOR TO WORK FOR YOU.
BUT WHEN IT COMES TO DETER-MINATION... BRYONY IS THE BEST.

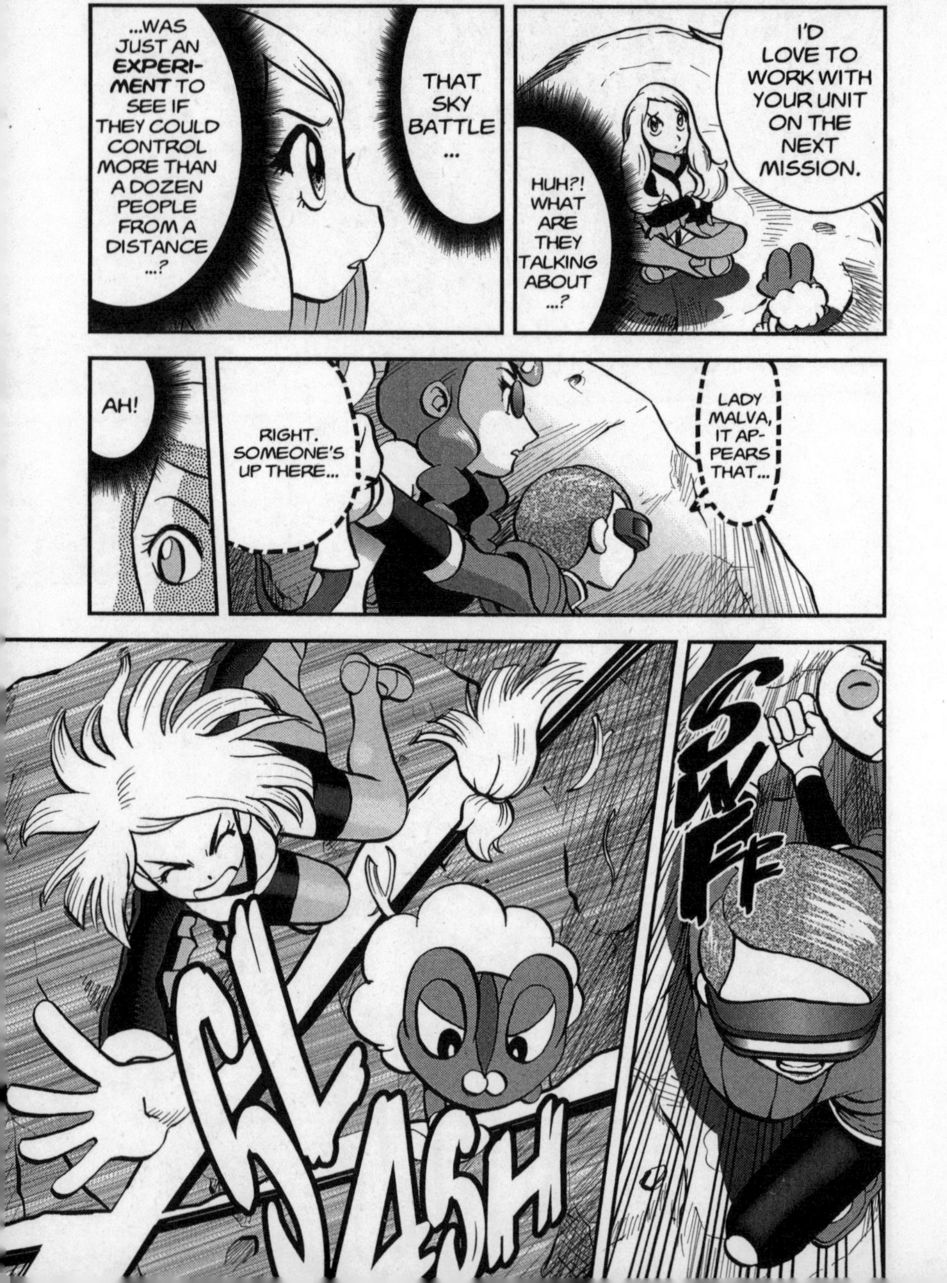
I'D LOVE TO WORK WITH YOUR UNIT ON THE NEXT MISSION.
HUH?! WHAT ARE THEY TALKING ABOUT ...?
THAT SKY BATTLE ...
...WAS JUST AN **EXPERIMENT** TO SEE IF THEY COULD CONTROL MORE THAN A DOZEN PEOPLE FROM A DISTANCE ...?
LADY MALVA, IT APPEARS THAT...
RIGHT. SOMEONE'S UP THERE...
AH!
SWFF
SLASH

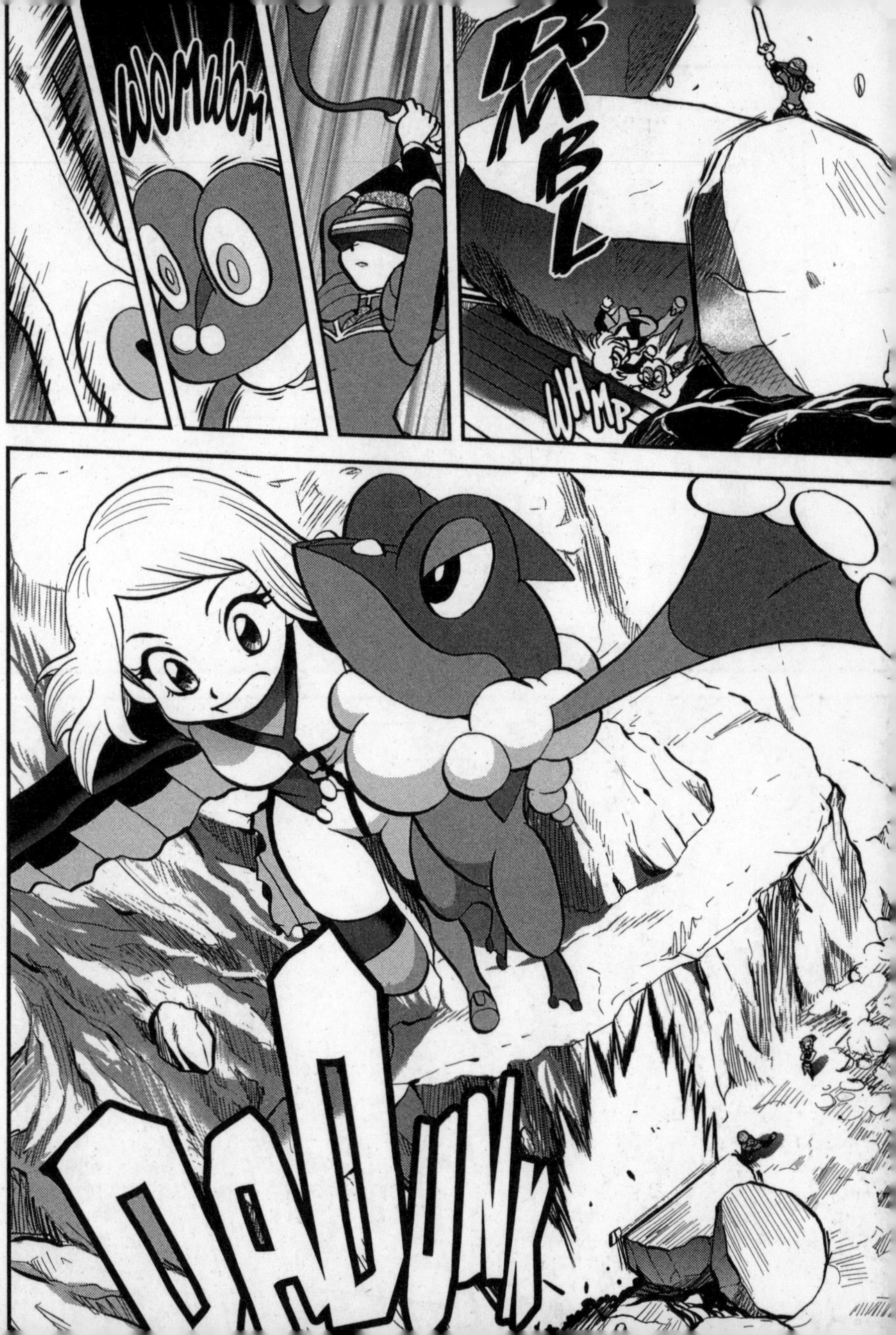
RUMBL
WHMP
WOMWOM
DADUNK

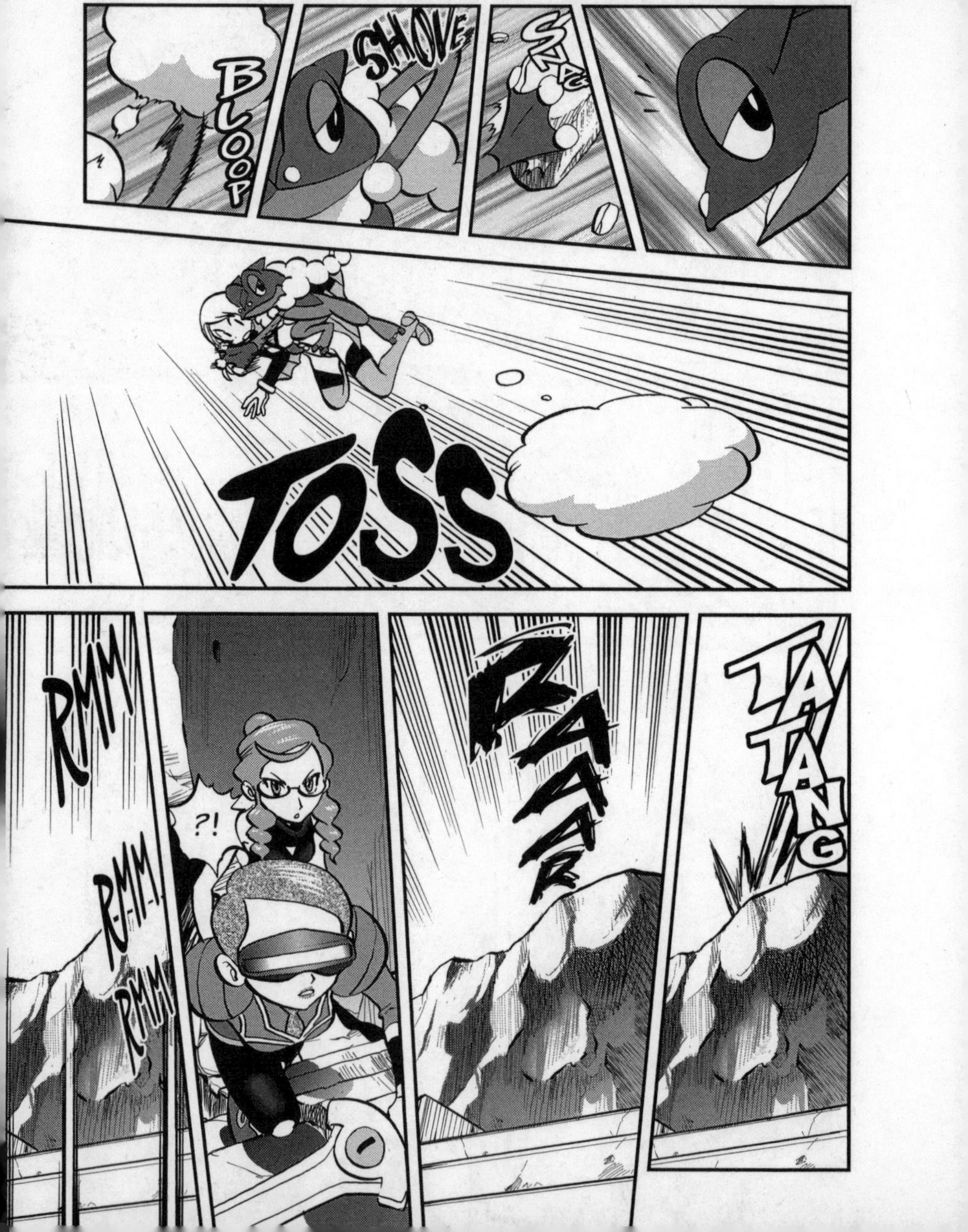

SNAG
SHOVE
BLOOP
TOSS
TATANG
RAAAA
?!
RMM
R-M-M-
RMM

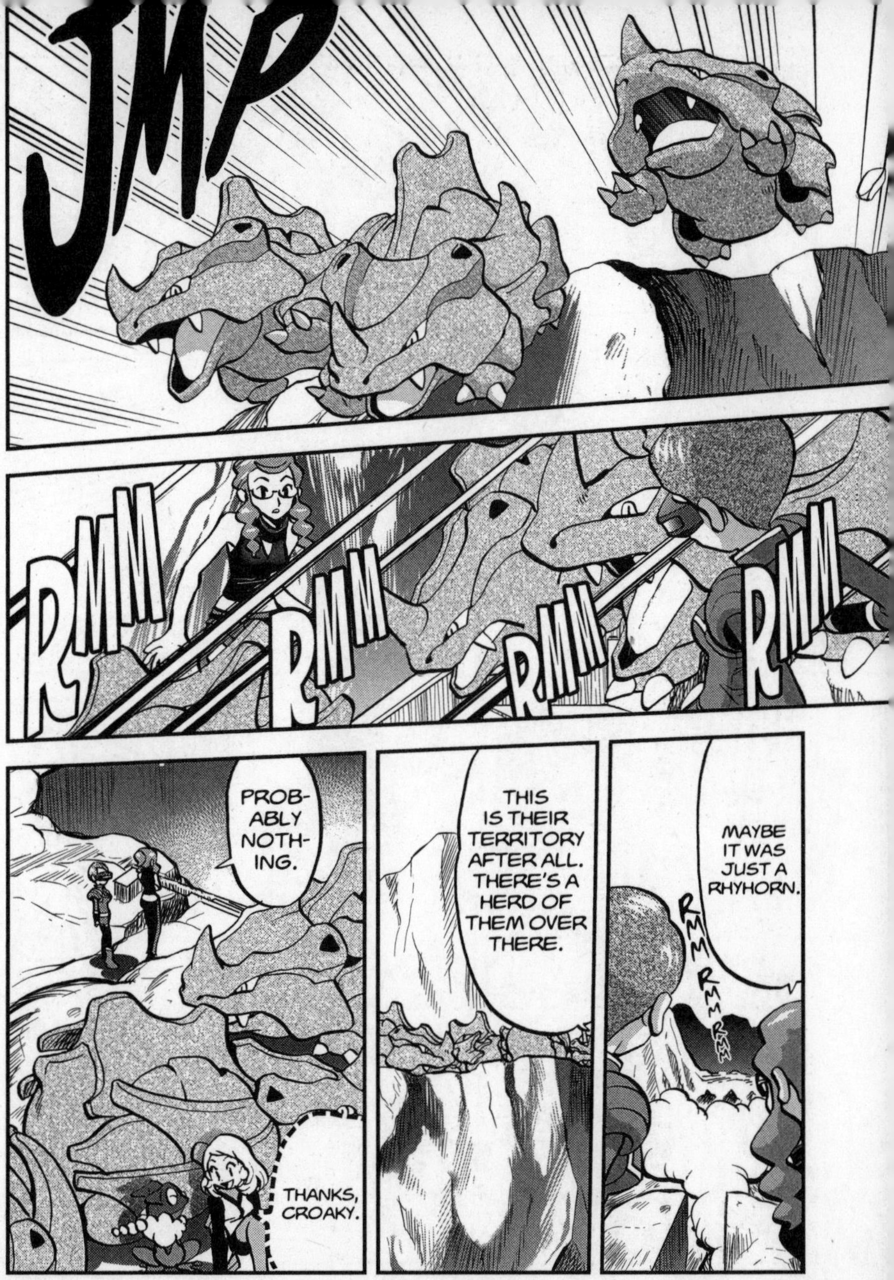
JMP
RMM
RMM
RMM
RMM
MAYBE IT WAS JUST A RHYHORN.
RMM RMM RMM
THIS IS THEIR TERRITORY AFTER ALL. THERE'S A HERD OF THEM OVER THERE.
PROB-ABLY NOTH-ING.
THANKS, CROAKY.

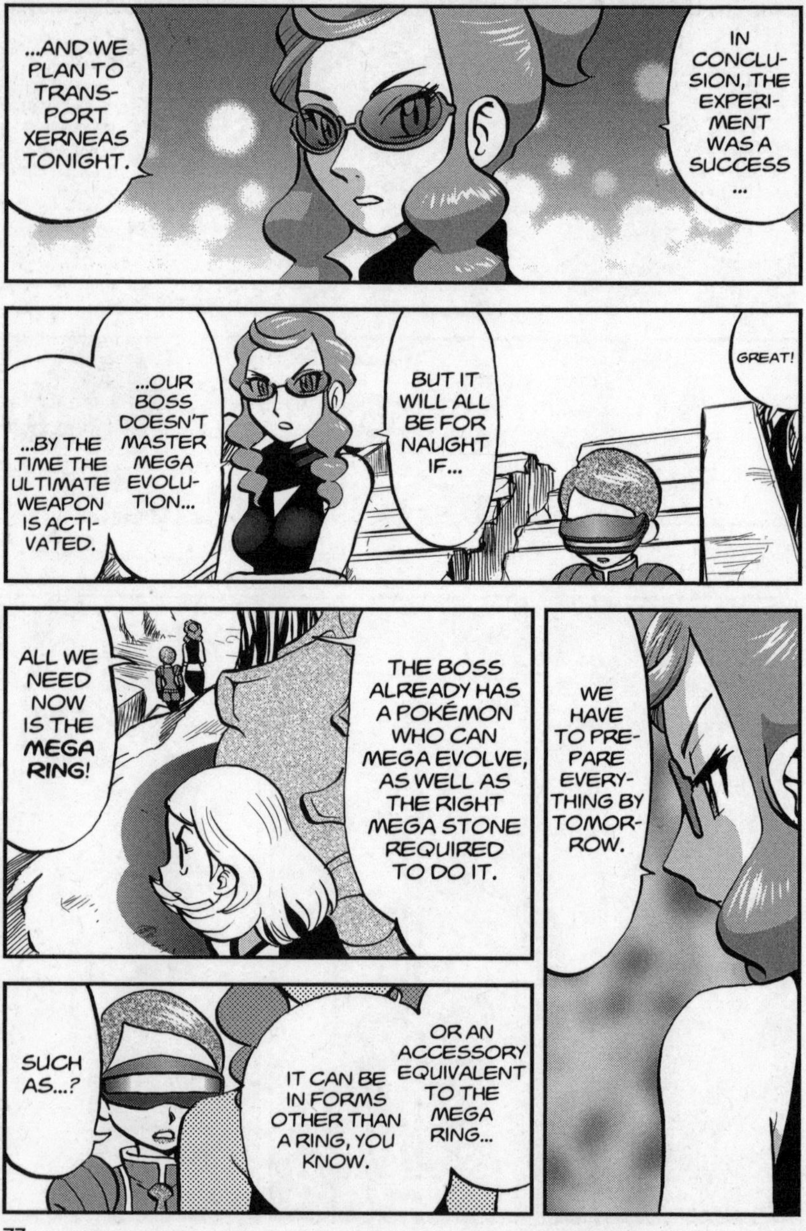
IN CONCLUSION, THE EXPERIMENT WAS A SUCCESS...
...AND WE PLAN TO TRANSPORT XERNEAS TONIGHT.
GREAT!
BUT IT WILL ALL BE FOR NAUGHT IF...
...OUR BOSS DOESN'T MASTER MEGA EVOLUTION...
...BY THE TIME THE ULTIMATE WEAPON IS ACTIVATED.
WE HAVE TO PREPARE EVERYTHING BY TOMORROW.
THE BOSS ALREADY HAS A POKÉMON WHO CAN MEGA EVOLVE, AS WELL AS THE RIGHT MEGA STONE REQUIRED TO DO IT.
ALL WE NEED NOW IS THE **MEGA RING**!
OR AN ACCESSORY EQUIVALENT TO THE MEGA RING...
IT CAN BE IN FORMS OTHER THAN A RING, YOU KNOW.
SUCH AS...?

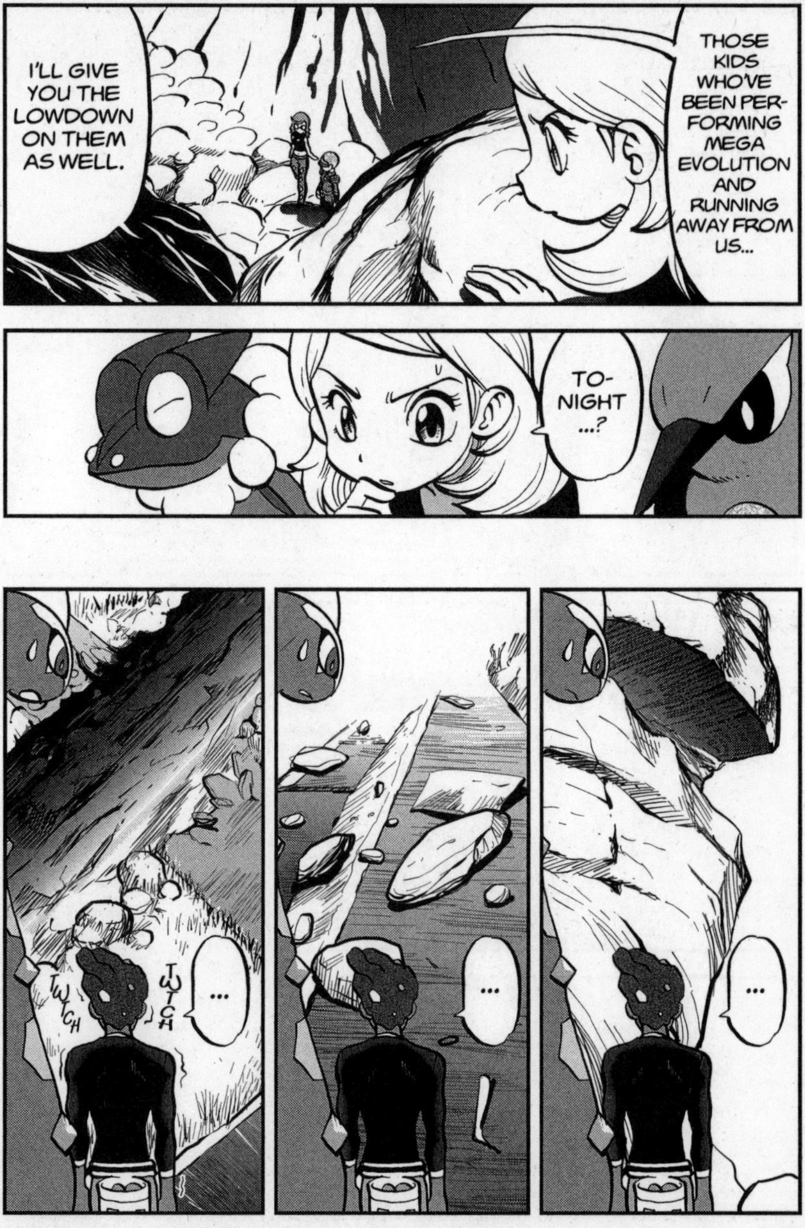
THOSE KIDS WHO'VE BEEN PER-FORMING MEGA EVOLUTION AND RUNNING AWAY FROM US...
I'LL GIVE YOU THE LOWDOWN ON THEM AS WELL.
TO-NIGHT ...?
...
...
...
TWITCH
TWITCH

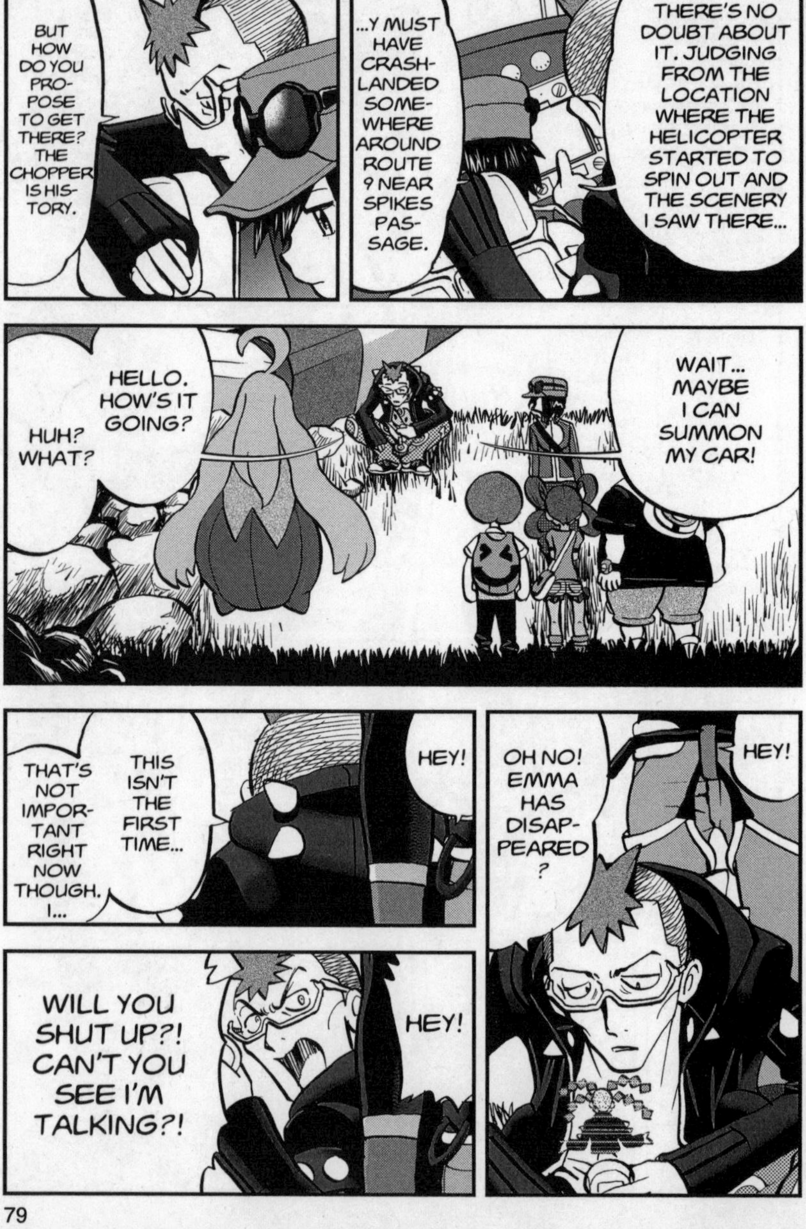
THERE'S NO DOUBT ABOUT IT. JUDGING FROM THE LOCATION WHERE THE HELICOPTER STARTED TO SPIN OUT AND THE SCENERY I SAW THERE...
...Y MUST HAVE CRASH-LANDED SOME-WHERE AROUND ROUTE 9 NEAR SPIKES PAS-SAGE.
BUT HOW DO YOU PRO-POSE TO GET THERE? THE CHOPPER IS HIS-TORY.
WAIT... MAYBE I CAN SUMMON MY CAR!
HELLO. HOW'S IT GOING?
HUH? WHAT?
HEY!
OH NO! EMMA HAS DISAP-PEARED?
HEY!
THIS ISN'T THE FIRST TIME...
THAT'S NOT IMPOR-TANT RIGHT NOW THOUGH. I...
HEY!
WILL YOU SHUT UP?! CAN'T YOU SEE I'M TALKING?!

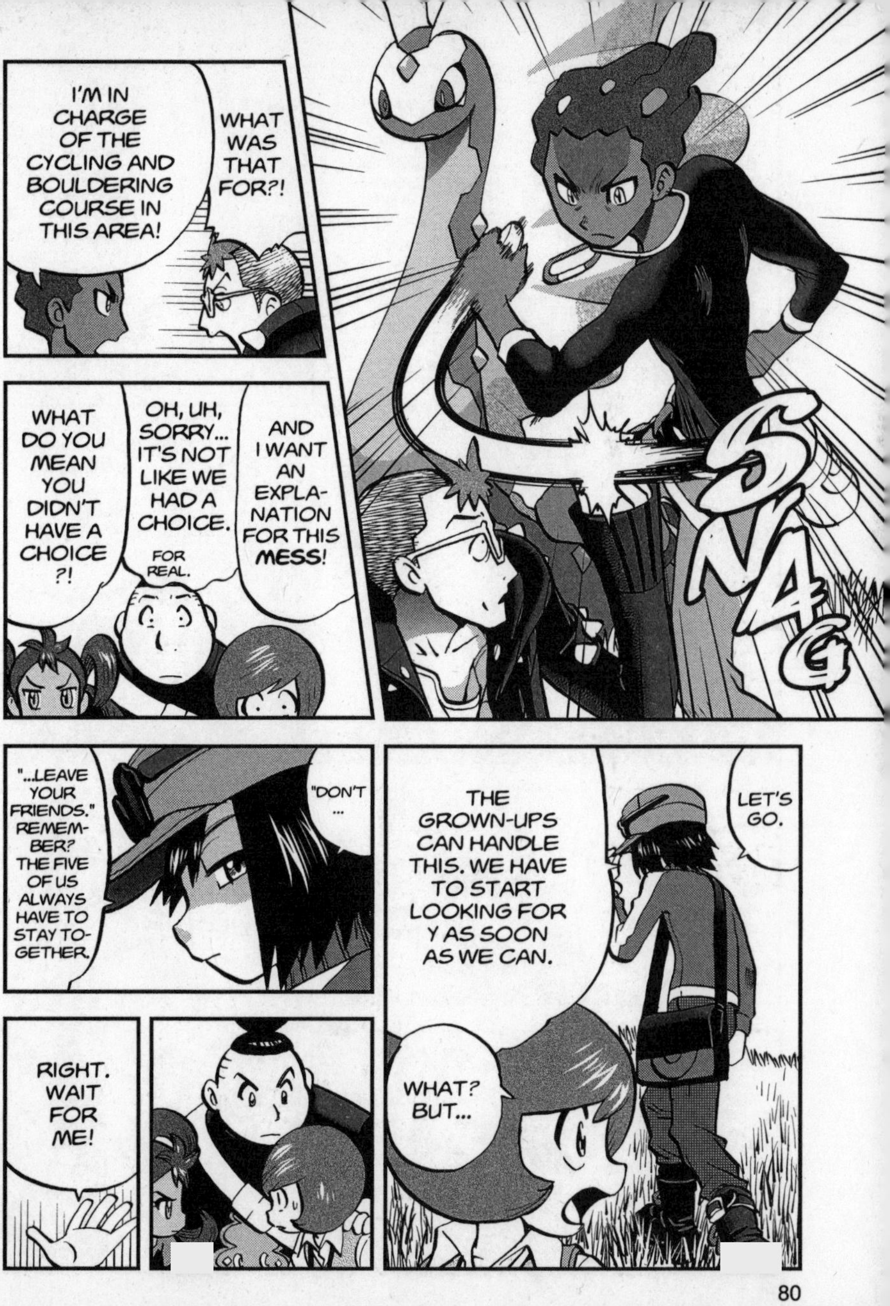
SNAG
WHAT WAS THAT FOR?!
I'M IN CHARGE OF THE CYCLING AND BOULDERING COURSE IN THIS AREA!
AND I WANT AN EXPLANATION FOR THIS MESS!
OH, UH, SORRY... IT'S NOT LIKE WE HAD A CHOICE.
FOR REAL.
WHAT DO YOU MEAN YOU DIDN'T HAVE A CHOICE?!
LET'S GO.
THE GROWN-UPS CAN HANDLE THIS. WE HAVE TO START LOOKING FOR Y AS SOON AS WE CAN.
"DON'T ...
"...LEAVE YOUR FRIENDS." REMEMBER? THE FIVE OF US ALWAYS HAVE TO STAY TOGETHER.
WHAT? BUT...
RIGHT. WAIT FOR ME!

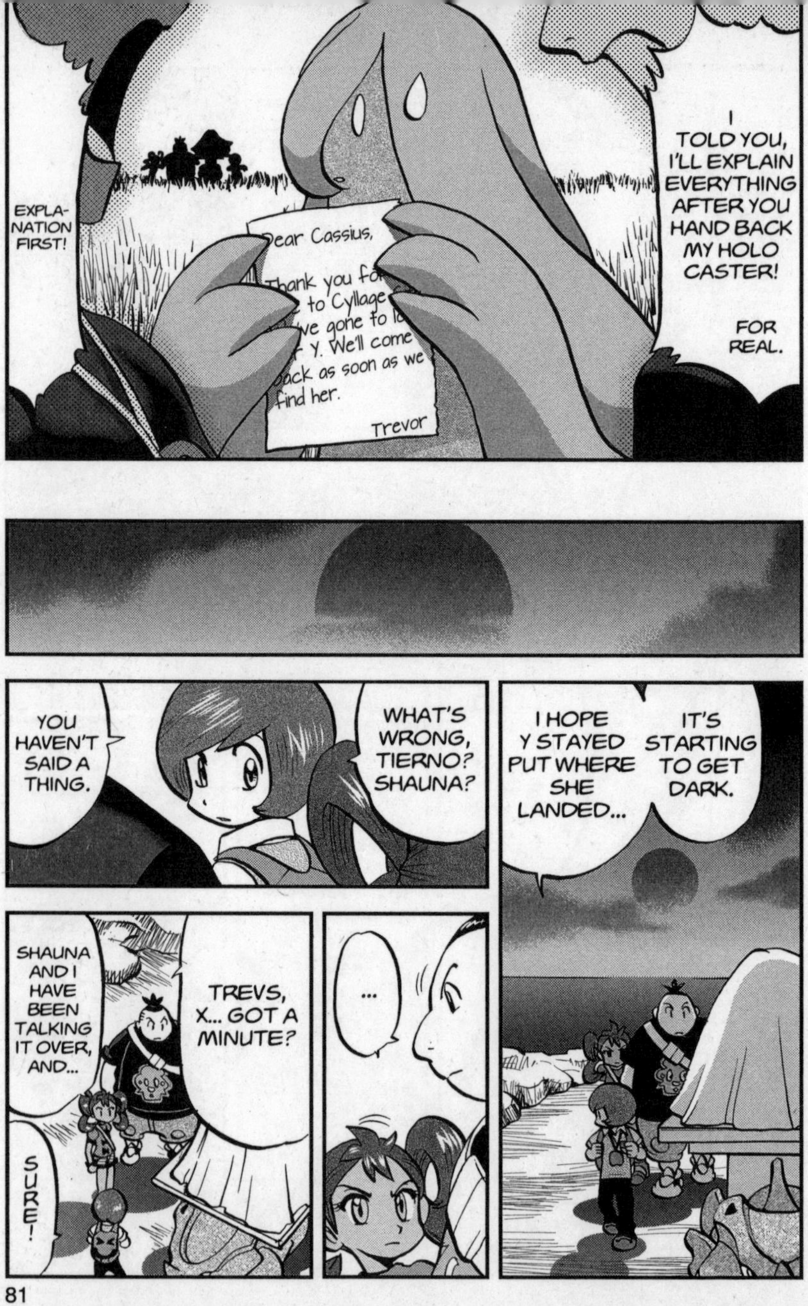
I TOLD YOU, I'LL EXPLAIN EVERYTHING AFTER YOU HAND BACK MY HOLO CASTER!
FOR REAL.
EXPLANATION FIRST!
Dear Cassius,
Thank you fo
to Cyllage
ve gone to lo
Y. We'll come
ack as soon as we
find her.
Trevor
IT'S STARTING TO GET DARK.
I HOPE Y STAYED PUT WHERE SHE LANDED...
WHAT'S WRONG, TIERNO? SHAUNA?
YOU HAVEN'T SAID A THING.
...
TREVS, X... GOT A MINUTE?
SHAUNA AND I HAVE BEEN TALKING IT OVER, AND...
SURE!

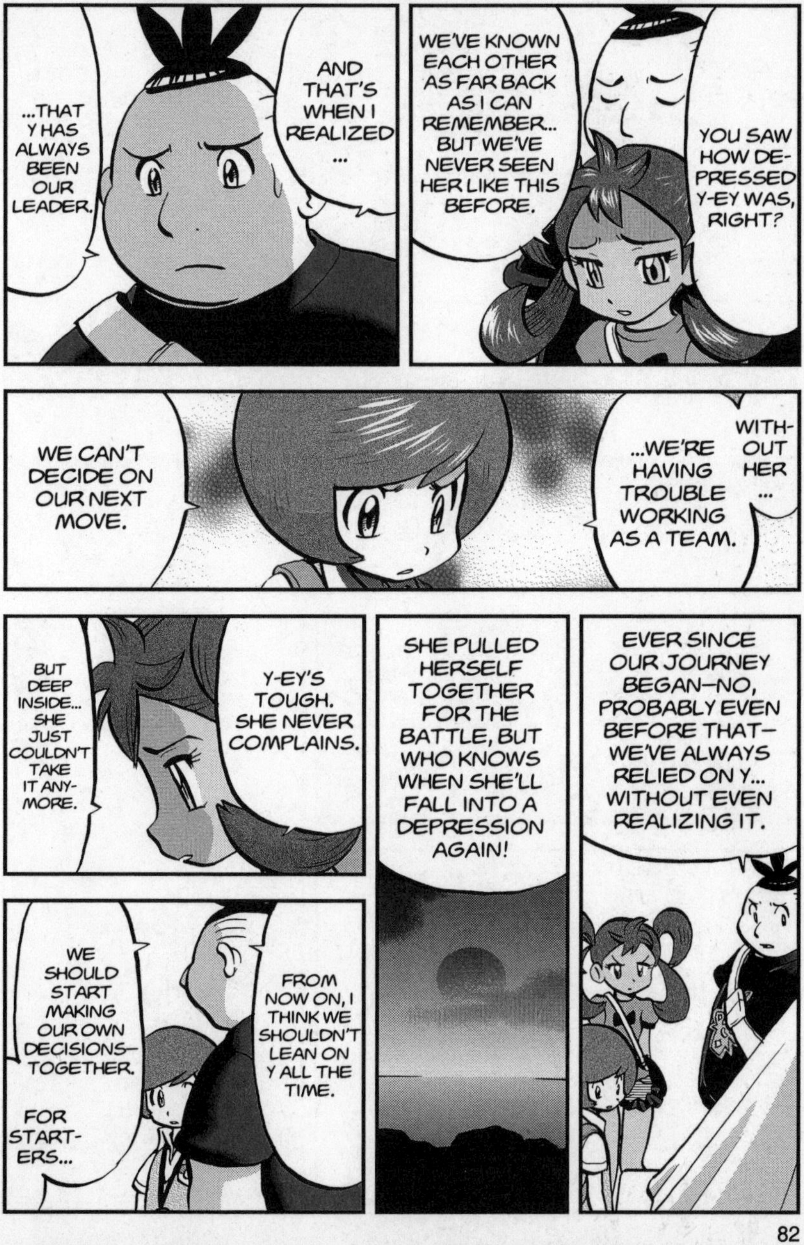
YOU SAW HOW DE-PRESSED Y-EY WAS, RIGHT?
WE'VE KNOWN EACH OTHER AS FAR BACK AS I CAN REMEMBER... BUT WE'VE NEVER SEEN HER LIKE THIS BEFORE.
AND THAT'S WHEN I REALIZED...
...THAT Y HAS ALWAYS BEEN OUR LEADER.
WITH-OUT HER...
...WE'RE HAVING TROUBLE WORKING AS A TEAM.
WE CAN'T DECIDE ON OUR NEXT MOVE.
EVER SINCE OUR JOURNEY BEGAN—NO, PROBABLY EVEN BEFORE THAT—WE'VE ALWAYS RELIED ON Y... WITHOUT EVEN REALIZING IT.
SHE PULLED HERSELF TOGETHER FOR THE BATTLE, BUT WHO KNOWS WHEN SHE'LL FALL INTO A DEPRESSION AGAIN!
Y-EY'S TOUGH. SHE NEVER COMPLAINS.
BUT DEEP INSIDE... SHE JUST COULDN'T TAKE IT ANY-MORE.
FROM NOW ON, I THINK WE SHOULDN'T LEAN ON Y ALL THE TIME.
WE SHOULD START MAKING OUR OWN DECISIONS—TOGETHER.
FOR START-ERS...

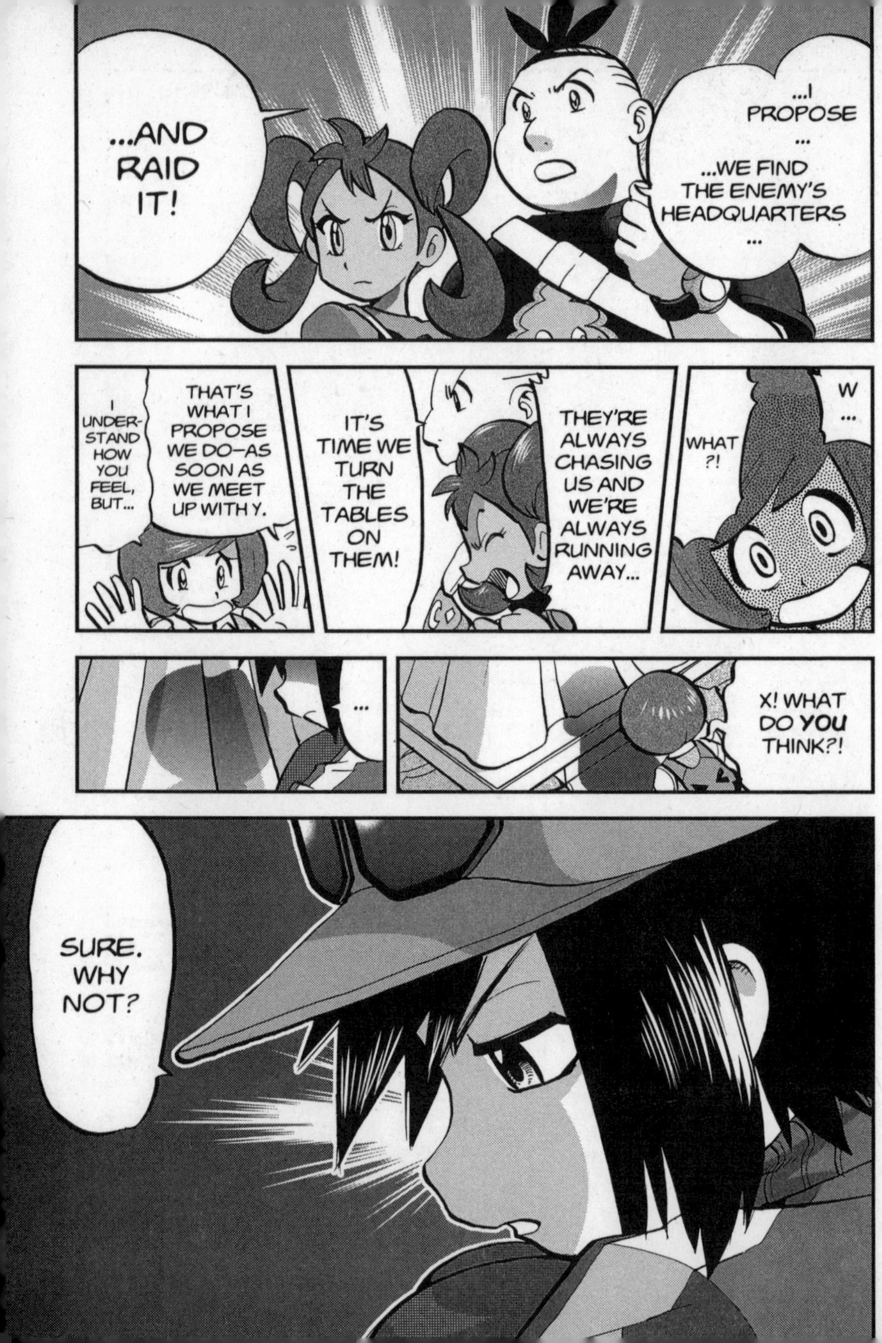
...I PROPOSE ... ...WE FIND THE ENEMY'S HEADQUARTERS ...
...AND RAID IT!
W ...
WHAT ?!
THEY'RE ALWAYS CHASING US AND WE'RE ALWAYS RUNNING AWAY...
IT'S TIME WE TURN THE TABLES ON THEM!
THAT'S WHAT I PROPOSE WE DO—AS SOON AS WE MEET UP WITH Y.
I UNDERSTAND HOW YOU FEEL, BUT...
X! WHAT DO **YOU** THINK?!
...
SURE. WHY NOT?

Current Location

Cyllage City

A city nestled between the cliffs and the sea, overlooked by steep Bicycle racecourses.

▼

**Route 8
Muraille Coast**

This is a road of great contrasts, from the harsh rock of the cliffs to the soft sands of the beach.

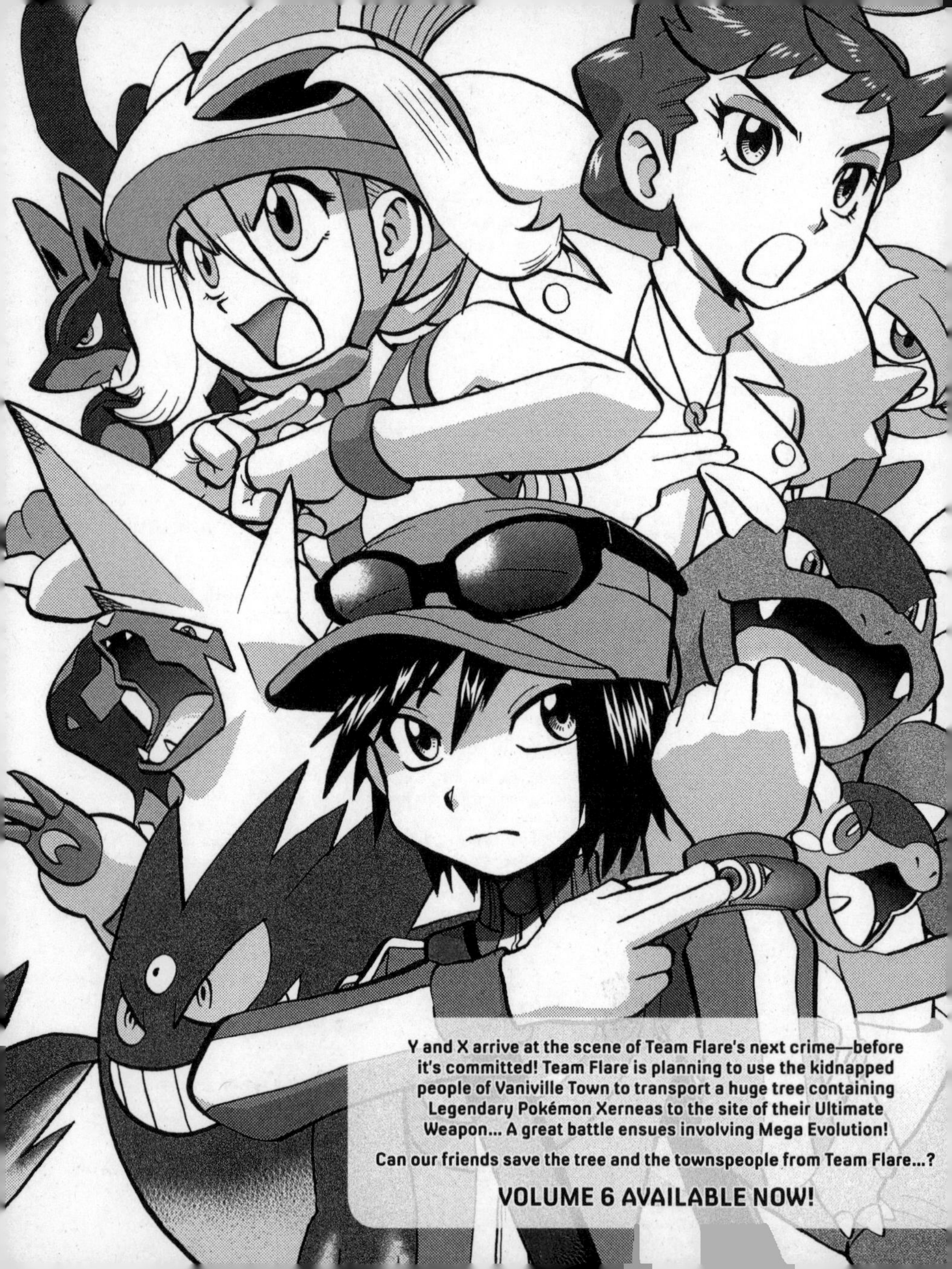
Y and X arrive at the scene of Team Flare's next crime—before it's committed! Team Flare is planning to use the kidnapped people of Vaniville Town to transport a huge tree containing Legendary Pokémon Xerneas to the site of their Ultimate Weapon... A great battle ensues involving Mega Evolution!
Can our friends save the tree and the townspeople from Team Flare...?
VOLUME 6 AVAILABLE NOW!

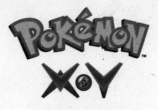

Pokémon X • Y
Volume 5
Perfect Square Edition

Story by HIDENORI KUSAKA
Art by SATOSHI YAMAMOTO

©2015 The Pokémon Company International.
©1995-2015 Nintendo/Creatures Inc./GAME FREAK inc.
TM, ®, and character names are trademarks of Nintendo.
POCKET MONSTERS SPECIAL X·Y Vol. 5
by Hidenori KUSAKA, Satoshi YAMAMOTO
© 2014 Hidenori KUSAKA, Satoshi YAMAMOTO
All rights reserved.
Original Japanese edition published by SHOGAKUKAN.
English translation rights in the United States of America, Canada, the United
Kingdom, Ireland, Australia and New Zealand arranged with SHOGAKUKAN.

English Adaptation—Bryant Turnage
Translation—Tetsuichiro Miyaki
Touch-up & Lettering—Annaliese Christman
Design—Shawn Carrico
Editor—Annette Roman

Printed in the U.S.A.

Published by
VIZ Media, LLC
P.O. Box 77010
San Francisco, CA 94107

10 9 8 7 6 5 4 3 2
First printing, December 2015
Second printing, October 2016

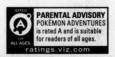

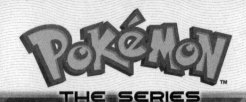
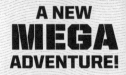

Begin your Pokémon Adventure here in the Kanto region!

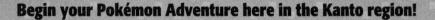

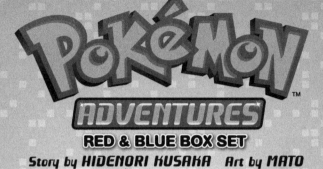

RED & BLUE BOX SET

Story by HIDENORI KUSAKA   Art by MATO

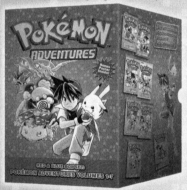

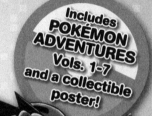

Includes **POKÉMON ADVENTURES** Vols. 1-7 and a collectible poster!

All your favorite Pokémon game characters jump out of the screen into the pages of this action-packed manga!

Red doesn't just want to train Pokémon, he wants to be their friend too. Bulbasaur and Poliwhirl seem game. But independent Pikachu won't be so easy to win over!

And watch out for Team Rocket, Red... They only want to be your enemy!

Start the adventure today!

VIZ MEDIA
www.viz.com

PERFECT SQUARE

RATED **A** FOR ALL AGES
ratings.viz.com

The adventure continues in the Johto region!

POKÉMON™ ADVENTURES

GOLD & SILVER BOX SET

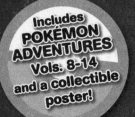

Includes POKÉMON ADVENTURES Vols. 8-14 and a collectible poster!

Pokémon ADVENTURES
GOLD & SILVER
Bonus Poster Inside!
GOLD & SILVER BOX SET:
POKÉMON ADVENTURES VOLUMES 8-14

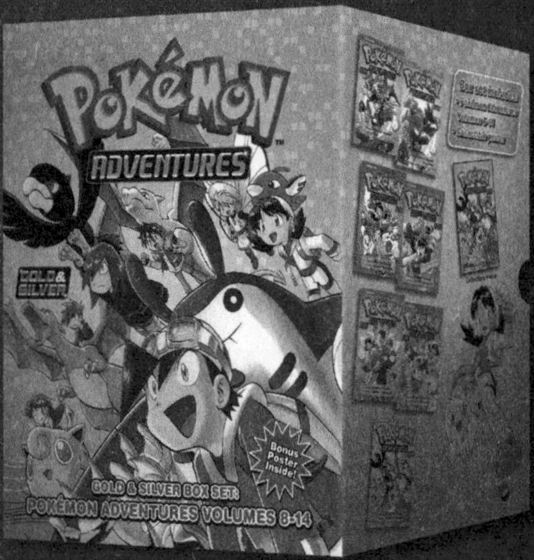

Story by
HIDENORI KUSAKA

Art by
MATO, SATOSHI YAMAMOTO

More exciting Pokémon adventures starring Gold and his rival Silver! First someone steals Gold's backpack full of Poké Balls (and Pokémon!). Then someone steals Prof. Elm's Totodile. Can Gold catch the thief—or thieves?!

Keep an eye on Team Rocket, Gold... Could they be behind this crime wave?

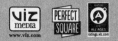

www.viz.com

RATED ALL AGES ratings.viz.com

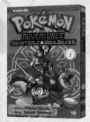
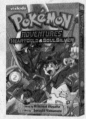

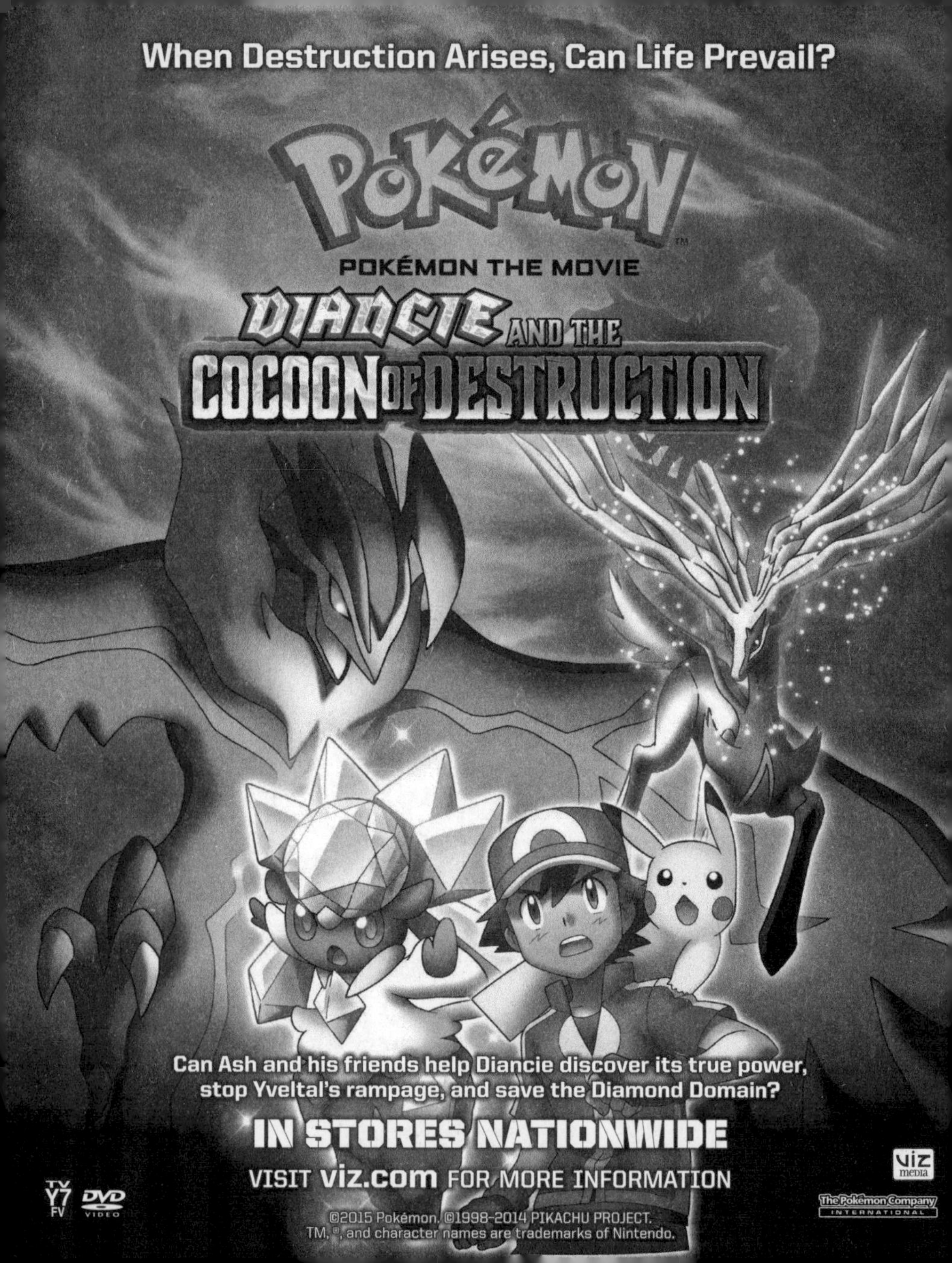
When Destruction Arises, Can Life Prevail?
POKÉMON
POKÉMON THE MOVIE
DIANCIE AND THE COCOON OF DESTRUCTION
Can Ash and his friends help Diancie discover its true power, stop Yveltal's rampage, and save the Diamond Domain?
IN STORES NATIONWIDE
VISIT viz.com FOR MORE INFORMATION
TV Y7 FV
DVD VIDEO
VIZ media
The Pokémon Company INTERNATIONAL
©2015 Pokémon. ©1998-2014 PIKACHU PROJECT.
TM, ®, and character names are trademarks of Nintendo.

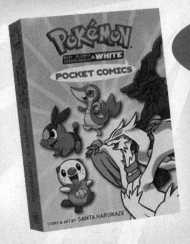

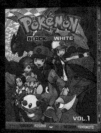
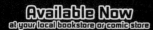

POKÉMON™

POCKET COMICS
Legendary Pokémon

STORY & ART BY SANTA HARUKAZE

MY FRIEND PIKACHU HASN'T BEEN SMILING RECENTLY...
grumph

THERE MUST BE A JOKE SOMEWHERE IN THIS WORLD THAT CAN BRING BACK PIKACHU'S SMILE!
THE LEGENDARY JOKE... IT'S UP TO ME TO FIND IT!

FOUR-PANEL GAGS, POKÉMON TRIVIA, AND FUN PUZZLES BASED ON THE CHARACTERS FROM THE BEST-SELLING POKÉMON BLACK AND WHITE VIDEO GAMES!

Available now!

POKÉMON
POCKET COMICS
Legendary Pokémon
STORY & ART BY SANTA HARUKAZE

To the forest! To the sea!
To Legendary Island!

Join our Pokémon pals on their quest through Unova—while testing your knowledge and laughing all the way!

Ask for it at your local comic book shop or bookstore!

ISBN: 978-1-4215-8128-6

RATED A ALL AGES ratings.viz.com

PERFECT SQUARE www.PerfectSquare.com

VIZ media www.viz.com

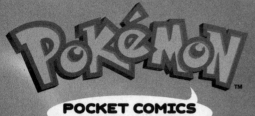

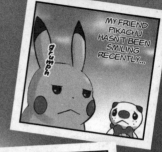

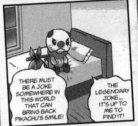

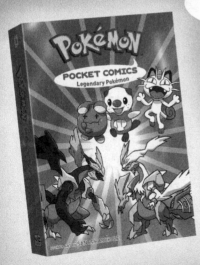

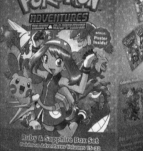
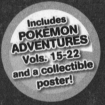
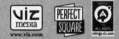

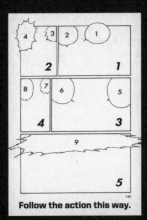

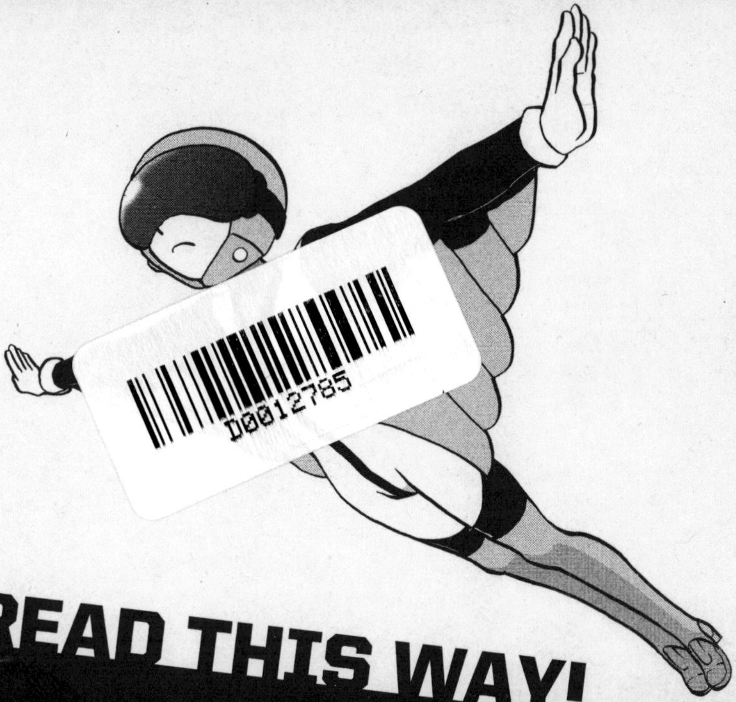

⟨⟨⟨ READ THIS WAY!

THIS IS THE END OF THIS GRAPHIC NOVEL!

To properly enjoy this VIZ Media graphic novel, please turn it around and begin reading from right to left.

This book has been printed in the original Japanese format in order to preserve the orientation of the original artwork. Have fun with it!

Follow the action this way.